J.M. HOLMES

FALLING FROM SPACE

A Kat & Jerry mystery

LITERATI INTERNATIONAL
~ SINCE 1981 ~
Toronto • New York • London

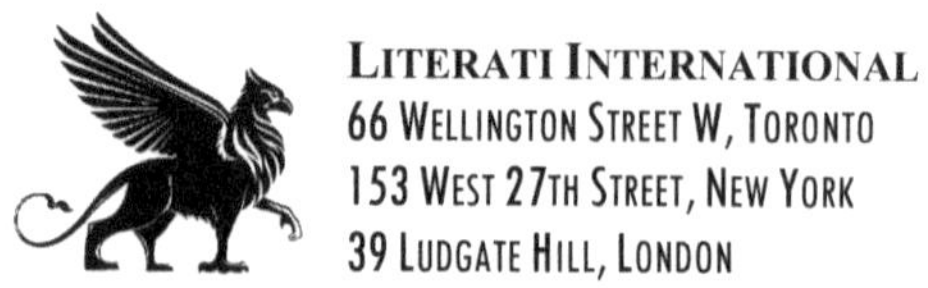

Library of Congress Control Number: 2021925486
ISBN 978-1-956784-18-3

Space Elevator

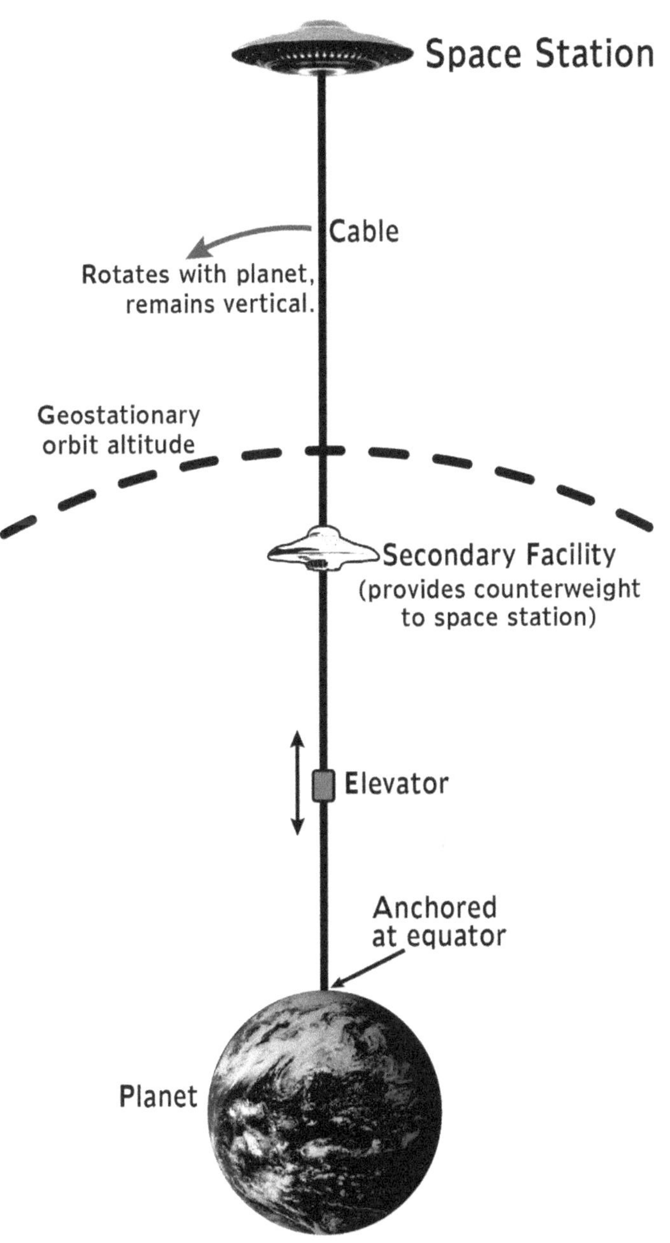

Also by J.M. Holmes:

Retrievers; A Kat & Jerry Anthology

Adventure in Asteroid City; A Kat & Jerry Mystery

Ice, Ice, Baby (*with* Prodigy *and* Time Trial)

They Left Me for Dead; A Crime Noir Thriller

Beautiful, Naked, Rich… and DEAD

A Deep Breath of Water

Little Potato Fries *(collected poems)*

Pro Tem: The Amazing Year *(nonfiction)*

Scan this code to view or purchase any of these books

All titles available in paperback, hardcover, and large print editions

for Sarahtops

the most difficult woman I know

MEET OUR HEROES

From the moment Kat meets Jerry, with her hands tied above her head as an assassin moves in for the kill, another of the galaxy's great love stories is born.

They're an unlikely duo: she a creature of the real Space Age, when cheap lightspeed travel is available to everyone; and he a product of the distant past, a former titan of industry revived from a regeneration tube, a man firmly rooted in the earthbound 20th century.

But, as the criminals, con men, assassins and treacherous partners who cross swords with them quickly learn, this pair of wisecracking, fearless sleuths – armed with nothing but their wits and a powerful quantum computer housed in Kat's eyeglasses – are formidable opponents with the sharpest minds this side of Alpha Centauri.

This book is a standalone, novel-length adventure featuring these two clever fortune-hunters whom many readers first met in the book, *"Retrievers"*, an anthology of their earliest exploits.

If this is your first time encountering Kat and Jerry, strap in and prepare for a wild ride as they solve mysteries, dodge bad guys, and fight for their lives. Enjoy!

falling from space

prologue

 **HEN YOU'RE PLUNGING** toward the ground at 12,000 mph, you can't help but feel a little nervous.

Jerry craned his neck to the left and tried to peer out the window, but he needn't have bothered. The intermittent sight of the cable was nothing but a blurred line streaking past his vision and offered no clues to his position or altitude.

But the brief glimpses of the tether were still comforting, nonetheless. They reassured him that he had not spun off into the ether, gliding away on the gradually thickening streaks of atmosphere that were only just now starting to buffet his vessel.

He had no idea where Kat was, and hoped her craft was also still bound to the nanofiber cable, but since he was powerless to assist her in any way he put her wellbeing out of his mind and focused on the task at hand.

The minimal instrument panel in front of him did little more than report his altitude and velocity, and right now both numbers were terrifying. As the altitude readout numerically decreased, the velocity readout reciprocally increased.

Jerry pressed himself back into the seat as firmly as he could. Even though he was resting on his back in a fully recumbent position, he knew that when the braking system kicked in, the G-forces would hit him with enough crushing power to break bones, if he wasn't perfectly positioned.

A tremendous roar began to scream through the tiny cabin as the craft forced its way down through the thickening atmosphere, and blinding flashes of light filled the cabin as the air outside ignited in compression.

Finally, the system reached its failsafe speed and the emergency braking kicked in. But either a faulty receptor or a flaw in the ship's design turned what should have been a stable, rapid deceleration into a jarring, spinning, twisting corkscrew of motion. Jerry felt the straps around his shoulders and chest cut deep into him as the craft gyrated out of control, alternately jerking his head down against his chest or slamming it back into the headrest.

Through the viewport he saw the craft's emergency chute deploy, and then was horrified to watch the twisting capsule tangle the chute's lines and inextricably wrap itself up in the fabric.

His began choking under a suffocating weight that crushed his ribs against his lungs. Finally, a violent spin rammed his head to the side and against the headrest support, and everything went black as he lost consciousness.

1

"**H**EY JERRY,** check this out, wouldja?"

Jerry looked up at Kat from his position on his back underneath their spaceship's dashboard. Little streaks of grease marked his face and hair, and perspiration was dripping along his temples.

"Can it wait, Kat? I'm in the middle of something here."

"Oh Jerry, why don't you just break down and hire a tech to do that? There's no shame in admitting you can't do literally everything, you know."

"So you think I'd be happier paying some wet-behind-the-ears kid 50 credits an hour to do something I can do equally well?"

"Hmm, well let's see…. You've been struggling with adjusting those controls for almost three hours now, you've skinned pretty-well every knuckle on both your hands, broken at least one fingernail – if the cursing sounds are any indication – and in the process managed to completely disable all the posture controls on the pilot's seat, but not before moving it into a position that only a circus contortionist could wedge into.

"So, yeah, I think the 50 credits sounds like a good deal."

Sighing heavily, Jerry pushed/pulled himself out from under the dash and slowly crawled to his feet, where he stood twisting his back and stretching out both arms, to the accompaniment of loud cracking, popping sounds from his aching joints.

"Maybe they should have replaced your bones with titanium struts, instead of just growing you new ones," said Kat, giggling at Jerry wincing as his stiff muscles loosened up.

"Har de har. I'll have you know, I've never been in better shape. I'm just used to more vigourous activities than being cramped up into a pretzel for hours at a time."

"Well, I hate to break it to you, o love of my life, but there may be a lot more pretzel time ahead for you. Have you seen what you did to your chair?"

Jerry looked over ruefully at his command chair, which was now positioned only inches away from the dash, with the seat- back viciously inclined forward and the seat base wedged at a tight 45 degrees under it.

"You can't blame me for that, Kat. The controls seem to have been reversed. I thought I was adjusting it out and back, but when I hit the juice it snapped into that position like a folding camp chair collapsing on itself. And then it died."

"Which is what you'll be doing if you so much as breathe in the direction of *my* chair, Jer."

They looked over at Kat's co-pilot chair, which reclined at a glorious angle indicating sumptuous comfort.

"Really, Kat? You don't get backaches in that position?"

Kat laughed wickedly and in answer flopped down and splayed out in decadent repose in her chair.

"Backaches should be the least of your concern, Jer. As it is now, we're going to have to find a shoe horn to get you in and out of your seat."

"Well, I might be willing to admit you're right. And since there are no podiatrist's tools handy, I'll just leave the driving to you while I go for a soak in the hot tub," said Jerry, exiting the cockpit.

"Hey! Not so fast!" hollered Kat, smacking her hand down on the autopilot as she launched herself out of her chair and through the cabin.

"I think I might have gotten a backache from my chair after all – I'd better join you for a therapeutic soak," she called out, pulling off her clothes and dropping them in a little trail behind her as she jogged after him and disappeared into the ship.

"AS MUCH AS I'm enjoying myself," said Jerry, lazily tracing with his toe the path of an errant drop of water meandering down the wall beside the hot tub, "we really need to get back underway, and maybe that furshlugginer chair of mine is beyond my ability to repair after all."

Kat made no response. Jerry glanced over at her in curiosity, but was greeted with the sight of a swirling, empty space.

"Kat?" he called out, puzzled how she could have made her escape without his noticing.

Before he could call out again, Kat's head burst out of the water as she flopped back against the lip of the hot tub.

"Ahhhhhh, Jerry, that was *such* a good idea including this tub in the ship's options," she purred, water streaming down her face and hair.

"Having a good time, are we?" asked Jerry, a wry grin on his face.

"I'll say! Now if only I could convince Batman to come sit on the edge beside me, I'd be happy as a clam."

Curled up on a carpeted pad by the tub, the little black and white cat looked up at the sound of his name. His ears swiveled forward slightly, listening intently for the phonetics which he had come to associate with the arrival of food. Hearing no such syllabic refrain, he resumed his previous activity of chewing on his paw and ignoring the humans.

"Maybe he'd be at your side if you were sporting some of that smoked salmon you gorged him on this morning. And don't bother denying it, either. I smelled his breath from fifteen feet away as soon as I came into the galley. It was as pungent as strolling through the Fulton Fish Market. If I'd put my ear to his snout, I could have heard the ocean.

"I'm sure I have no idea what you're talking about," said Kat quietly.

"Look, I *know* you passed him the goods, Kat. Unless you'd like to contend that he's grown opposable thumbs and has learned how to open the walk-in freezer.

"Or are you sticking to your story that, one night, soused to the gills on cheap wine, I consumed, all by myself, the entire supply of lox we scored on Juneau Prime? And that I then passed out and purged the entire episode from my recollection?"

"I don't blame you for that -- I can't say as I'd want to remember such a debauched excursion into gluttony, either."

"Nice try, Kat, but I think the real explanation has to do with our little bet earlier over who could get Batman to come when we called him.

"Now I understand why he virtually hurled himself at you. A school of piranhas doesn't descend on their prey with half as much vigour. Obviously, associating yourself with large portions of seafood weighted the scales in your favour, and I have to say, I'm extremely disappointed you stooped to such unscrupulous tactics."

"Oh, shush, Jerry. You're just mad he likes me better."

"In your dreams, babe."

"Speaking of which, I'm thinking about taking a little nap in my copilot's chair – have you given any further thought to what you're going to do with your command chair?"

"Well, a few minutes ago while you were playing Jacques Cousteau, I was saying I'm ready to wave the white flag and get a professional to fix my chair."

"Wait wait, don't tell me – famous chef? Racecar driver? Fashion designer?"

"Wrong on all counts. World-renowned oceanographer."

"Well, maybe in *your* world, Jerry, not mine."

"Whatever. Not important. But I'm trying to tell you I'm willing to pass the baton to get the thing fixed."

"Groovy!" replied Kat, "Should we call the yacht company or are you going to find someone in the … brown pages?"

"*Yellow.* Yellow Pages. Brown is what happens to your pants when you see the bill.

"And no, it just so happens I know a guy."

"Of *course* you do. Why did I even—"

"He's a couple systems over," continued Jerry, "working on a planet I've been wanting to visit for a long time now."

"Is there something special about it? Exotic animals? Incredible landscapes? Maybe populated solely by Amazonian supermodels?"

"That last one sounds great, but unfortunately, none of the above. It's famous for an attraction not quite as glamourous, but no less fascinating – it happens to boast the only actual working Space Elevator in our universe. In any universe, for that matter."

"A Space Elevator! But I thought those were prohibitively expensive to build?"

"You're right, but this planet's got one. I've been wanting to see it ever since I first read about it, but the planet's a little off the beaten path, so I've never had the opportunity to drop by.

"But a former shipmate of mine is the chief engineer on the planetside end of the Elevator. We can dock at the spaceport at the top of the Elevator and ride it down to the surface to visit my buddy while he has one of his techs look at my chair."

"That sounds awesome Jerry! Finally! A real honest-to-goodness vacation with no guns or bad guys or dead cats to plague us!"

And with that, Kat disappeared once again beneath the water, as Jerry rolled his eyes and chuckled.

2

KAT RELEASED the ship's nav controls to the space station's computer and relaxed, reclining in her chair. The station's AI guided them into a berth beside a short-hop transport carrier emblazoned with the words: *Arrow Deliveries – The fastest line between any two points!* Beneath the slogan was a cartoon image of a spaceship with a delivery man smiling and waving while sticking his head out the ship's cockpit window.

As their ship settled to a stop, a shrill voice barked out at them from their console, *"Attention visitors! Do not attempt to exit your ship! Wait for an attendant to escort you to the Clearance Center! Repeat! Do not attempt …."* And the message repeated, for probably the fiftieth time since Kat had made contact with the facility after entering the planet's orbit.

"They take their security seriously around here," muttered Kat, warily eyeing the ships lined up along the docking bays.

"For what it cost to build this setup, I can't say I blame them," replied Jerry, peering out the viewport.

"Say, Jerry, what about Batman? Are we bringing him with us? He might get lonely if we're gone for several days."

"I doubt that," replied Jerry, watching as the cat rolled over on its carpeted perch behind the pilot's chair and then splayed out on its back in decadent repose. "What with his cat wheel and robotic mice to play with, he probably won't even notice we're gone. And since you went and got him an automatic feeder, water fountain, and self-cleaning litter box, the only thing he needs us for is to scratch him behind the ears and clean up his hairballs."

"Well, okay, but in case something unexpected happens to us, I'm scheduling an alert to the station if we're not back in a month – I wouldn't want him to starve to death in here."

After around fifteen minutes, and about three minutes before Kat was going to smash their squawking console speakers to pulp with a hammer, an officious-looking fellow dressed all in white in a vaguely naval military uniform strode up to their ship. He stood about ten feet away and tapped studiously on a small tablet before moving over to their entry port and knocking. The tablet must have sent an all-clear signal, because the cacophonous message abruptly stopped yammering out of their console speakers.

"Hello, Sir," he said with a broad smile as Jerry swung open the pressure door. "Welcome to Heaven's Gate Spaceport! We're happy to have you here and so sorry to make you wait. Don't take it personally – we have pretty tight security here, and everyone gets the same treatment, but now that I'm here we can get you debarked and processed through Clearance and done with all the red tape.

"My name's Ensign Holloway. Please follow me. And if you have any luggage, bring it with you now. Your ship's going to be sealed as soon as you leave it and you can't reenter it until you're ready to leave orbit, I'm sorry to say.

"Oh – and absolutely no firearms or weapons of any kind are allowed, of course, nor is any consumable item – that includes all foods, beverages, and smoking supplies. And if you have any medications you take, we'll need to see those, as well."

"Can we at least keep our clothing on or do we have to turn that over, too?" asked Jerry with a grin.

"Ha! Good one, Sir! No, clothing items are just fine – as long as you can't eat them."

"Darn. I guess you'll have to bring your non-edible underwear, Kat."

"Shucks. Some honeymoon this is going to be."

Ensign Holloway led them through the cavernous docking hangar until they came to a large pair of pressure doors set into the interior bulkhead, marked with a notice that they were entering the Clearance Center.

Both Kat and Jerry had been through Customs and Border Control screenings on dozens of other planets, but those previous experiences paled in comparison with the rigorous examination the station put them through.

First, their luggage was opened and emptied, with every toiletry item and garment individually scanned and visually examined. Seemingly at random, at least half their toiletries were plucked out and tossed into a large refuse bin behind the screeners.

Kat was fully expecting to be given grief over her Slimlines, but to her surprise they elicited barely a raised eyebrow. They went through the scanner, of course, but the examiner just nodded appreciatively at the fine workmanship of the design, and handed them back to Kat, who almost snatched them in relief, and jammed them back on her face.

Jerry and Kat themselves were each thoroughly scanned, first with a handheld scanner, then in a huge walk-in unit, and then physically patted-down by a human. They had to open their mouths and pull up their lips so their gums could be examined, and raise their tongues to show that nothing was concealed beneath them. The examiners ran gloved fingers through their hair, shone flashlights into their ears and up their noses, and squeezed them in several places a lot more intimately than seemed necessary.

But thankfully, after twenty minutes of probing, prodding and patting, they were given a clean pass and welcomed into the space station.

"Good Lord, that was intense," said Kat, as she carefully refolded their clothing at a side table generously provided to assist arrivals in repacking their dissected luggage. "The longer it went on the more I expected the full body-cavity search."

"Yeah, that crossed my mind, too, Kat, but I suppose the Powers That Be must have decided that's a bridge too far -- at least until they have a reason not to trust you."

"Amen to that. Remind me not to incur their wrath."

Once repacked, they moved to an exit door in the wall and stepped out into the space station proper.

It was a gigantic affair, a huge open space that curved off to either side in an arc that extended far past the range of their vision. Jerry and Kat were standing at the edge of an endless broad concourse that included shops, restaurants, various business services, and hotels.

Little electric carts carrying people or cargo whizzed back and forth, deftly avoiding the masses of humanity that moved through the space; some were obvious tourists and others business travelers, along with a variety of station personnel.

"What a huge operation," said Kat. "Look, you can see people coming out of dozens of other doors stretching away out of sight, and no doubt they've all been examined just as thoroughly as we were. If the rest of the station is like this, there must be at least a hundred thousand people in this facility."

"And that's just on this level. There are twenty more levels, with offices, shipping facilities, repair depots, you name it," said Jerry thoughtfully. "After all, it's the sole point of arrival and departure for an entire planet, and that includes all the people from hundreds of other worlds who come here to do business. I suppose keeping us waiting in our ship for only fifteen minutes was pretty efficient, after all."

"Yeah, so what's the story there," said Kat as they set off in a random direction. "I've never seen a planet before that didn't allow orbital craft to travel through their atmosphere."

"I'm not sure, hon. But I'll bet my buddy on the ground can explain it to us. Let's see if we can find the liaison point where he wants us to report."

3

AT'S GLASSES linked up with the station's Welcome Desk and displayed the route to their destination, which was an hour's walk away. They were only too delighted to stroll through the concourse after being cooped-up in their ship for the last several days.

They'd made it only halfway through their trek when Jerry yanked Kat so hard she almost lost her balance.

"Kat! Look!"

"Um, tell me what I'm supposed to be looking at – are you referring to that restaurant? What is… 'Benihana'?"

"I'll tell you what it is – it's where you and I will be spending the next two hours, that's what. And please don't call it a restaurant. It's as much a restaurant as your Slimlines are just a pair of eyeglasses."

"Wow, Jerry, I haven't seen you this excited since I wore that French maid outfit for Halloween on the Haunted Planet."

"And if they'd had a Benihana on that planet, you could have driven a stake through my heart right then and there and I'd have died happy. C'mon, let me show you one of the best things that ever came out of the twentieth century."

The meal was everything Jerry had hoped for. Kat was spellbound by the knife-tossing chef and his culinary acrobatics, while Jerry sat back and took in the show with a misty look in his eye. When they'd eaten their fill, reluctant to leave, they relocated to a table at the front of the restaurant where they could gaze out at the station concourse over a low row of window-box hedges.

About three bottles of sake in, Kat said, "So this is the life of a 21st century captain of industry. Doesn't seem so bad to me."

"Hey, this was the one and only indulgence I allowed myself, mostly because it was a good place to conduct business, especially after hours. You wouldn't believe the contracts people will sign at the end of an evening spent in a place like this."

"And I suppose you teetotaled, so you could be even more rapacious in your wheeling and dealing."

"I resent that remark. I was never rapacious."

"Of course not. I'm sure you amassed a fortune large enough to buy Manhattan by being a humanitarian philanthropist."

"You can't make an omelet without breaking a few eggs, Kat. I wasn't bargaining with Tibetan monks – most of the people I did business with were so ruthless they made me look like Mother Teresa in comparison."

As Kat opened her mouth, Jerry cut her off by saying, "Famous nun. Worked with the poor in India."

"Exactly the image I had in mind. The great Jerome, giant of the boardroom, dressed in a cassock, on his way to volunteer at the local soup kitchen. I can see it now: you and the other nuns, braiding each other's hair, telling inspirational stories about your day spent embracing lepers and helping old ladies cross the street."

"Not even close, Kat – leprosy was eradicated before I was out of high school."

"And autonomous cars eliminated pedestrian deaths, too, Jerry. But I still don't see you as the spiritual, giving type. At least, not then. Maybe you've softened in your old age. Or should I say, *very* old age."

Jerry just curled his lip at her, but Kat didn't notice, as she was paying careful attention to her hands as she refilled their glasses.

"Exactly why *did* you decide to regenerate, Jerry? Judging by everything you've told me, the life you lived sounds like a pretty empty experience: sixteen-hour days, two weeks a year for vacation – quite likely against your will and counting the hours till you could be back in the office – no family, probably no real friends…. Doesn't sound like an experience someone would want to spend billions to prolong, let alone repeat."

"You just answered your own question, Kat. Even I could see that I'd wasted almost two centuries of life in a meaningless quest for the almighty dollar. I didn't want to *repeat* my life. I wanted a *new* one, a redo, where I could have all the things I'd rejected my first time round – a family, good friends, time spent doing nothing but looking at the stars or snoozing in a hammock while my kids splashed around in the backyard pool."

"Stop already. I'm getting misty-eyed. And tell me: how's that new life been working out for you?"

"Well, for one, I've got a girlfriend now. True, she's a royal pain in the butt sometimes, but beggars can't be choosers, right?"

Kat just barked out a short laugh then drained her glass.

"And how about you, O Mistress of the Adumbral Void? What led you to become a space explorer in one of the loneliest professions known to man?"

"Escape, I suppose," she said as she waved at a waiter with the empty sake bottle.

"I'd just gone through a series of disastrous relationships when my uncle died and left me a spaceship. I was kind of flattered that he'd chosen to give it to me. I think he saw something in me that I hadn't realised myself.

"But I took it as a sign that the universe was telling me to vamoose to where there was no danger of accidentally starting another relationship."

"And how has *that* been working out for you, babe?" asked Jerry with a twinkle in his eyes.

"It's a work in progress. A lot like my current boyfriend."

The waiter arrived with a fresh bottle of sake and refilled their glasses while Kat sat quietly, sunk in reflection.

"You've never told me about those other boyfriends of yours, Kat. Were those relationships really that bad?"

"Complete train wrecks. I suppose I was just attracted to the wrong kind of guy. Over and over again."

"I didn't know you had a 'type' – tell me about them."

"Well, let's see…. They were controlling."

"I would never let you date someone like that."

"Self-centered."

"That reminds me of a story. When I was younger—"

"Intolerant and prejudiced."

"I hate those people."

"Violent."

"Makes me want to punch them in the face."

"Cheap."

"Did I mention we're going Dutch on this lunch?"

"Passive-aggressive."

"Feel free to polish-off that bottle by yourself, Kat – I can always flag down the waiter if I want to drink, too."

"Opinionated and judgmental."

"Look at that woman's outfit – did she cut up her drapes to make those clothes?"

"Needy. Manipulative. Demanding."

"When you're done talking I could really use a neck-rub, Kat. I promise I'll make it worth your while. I insist."

Kat looked at Jerry through slitted eyes.

"Nice try, Jer, but you're not getting out of this relationship that easy. And didn't you say something about flagging down the waiter for another bottle…?"

KAT WAS DRAINING the last of their fifth bottle when she noticed that Jerry was spending more and more time looking over her shoulder at something behind her.

"I know I'm not wearing a French maid outfit," she slurred, "but do you think you could pay just a teensy bit more attention to me than you are right now? I'm starting to feel like I'm just getting in the way of something more interesting."

"Hmm? Oh, sorry, Kat," said Jerry distractedly. "I didn't mean to be rude, but there's a woman behind you who hasn't stopped staring at me since the moment we sat down. If she were just giving me the eye, that would be one thing. But she's been focused in on me like a laser beam and it's giving me the creeps. And I can't say for certain, but I don't think she was here when we arrived – she may have actually followed us in."

Kat turned around, slowly, deliberately, but not discreetly at all, and brought her gaze to bear on the woman seated about five tables away.

She was all alone at a small table at the other side of the restaurant, nursing a glass of sake. She was elegantly dressed in a low-cut strapless red dress slit up to her hip, displaying an impressive length of shapely leg terminating in fiery red stiletto heels that matched her dress, lipstick, and nails. A shimmering expanse of raven-coloured tresses cascaded over her shoulders, framing large brown eyes in an almond-shaped face. As she kept staring at them Kat cursed quietly under her breath.

"That's real *cojones*, Jerry," she said, using one of his expressions. "She didn't even blink when I gave her the evil eye. It's as though I'm invisible."

Kat started to pull herself up off the banquette, turning in the other woman's direction.

"Well, let's see how invisible she thinks I am when I've got my hand around her thro—"

"Down, girl," said Jerry, gripping Kat by the shoulder and gently pushing her back down into her seat. "I don't know much about space stations, but I'll bet on this one they frown upon visitors disabling their fellow travelers.

"Let's wait some more and see how this plays out. I have a feeling something's going to happen sooner rather than later."

And sure enough, at that moment the woman stood up, laid a banknote on the table and moved toward the door.

"There. See? She's leaving. No harm, no foul."

But Jerry spoke too soon, for the woman walked past the door and made a beeline toward their table.

"Uh-oh," muttered Jerry under his breath. This didn't bode well.

"I need to sit down for a moment," said the woman, without preamble, as soon as she was standing beside their table. And without waiting for a response from Jerry or Kat, she squeezed down onto the banquette beside Jerry and sat there, hands in her lap, looking into his eyes.

"Now just one cotton-pickin' minute, lady—" began Kat, but before she could continue, the woman said, in a quiet whisper, "Shh! Please don't call attention to us. We're all in great danger."

"Well, *you* are for sure, I can tell you that," said Kat, picking up a salt shaker and starting to wrap a napkin around it.

"There, now, Kat. What have we learned about maiming fellow travelers?" said Jerry soothingly, gently taking the salt shaker out of Kat's hand and patting her clenched fist.

"You have to listen to me – we don't have much time," continued the woman in a frantic whisper. "I wasn't sure it was you until I saw your watch. And then I had to be sure we're not being surveilled."

Jerry glanced down at his wrist – he was wearing an antique Patek Philippe wristwatch made in the 1930's. He tended to forget he had it on, and regarded it more as a quaint piece of jewelry than as a utilitarian object. Probably not more than one in a hundred thousand people still wore wristwatches, but for Jerry it was a link to his former life, and to wear it brought him comfort, like hearing a song learned in childhood.

"My… watch?" said Jerry hesitantly. "Are you sure you're not confusing me with someone else? What has my watch got to do with anything?"

The woman looked at Jerry with horror in her eyes.

"You mean… you mean you're not my contact? Your watch – it's just a watch? You don't have the data disk?"

"I'm sorry, miss, but you have me at a disadvantage. I have no idea wh—"

Jerry's thought was cut off by a loud shout coming from the concourse outside the restaurant. A man was running along the transitway, followed by several beefy security guards who were calling out various commands and waving threatening-looking devices in his general direction. A crush of people emerging from a debarkation port prevented the security men from firing at the running man, but just as he drew even with Jerry's position in the restaurant, he failed to look to his left and ran straight into the path of a speeding trolley loaded with luggage. The trolley hit him full-on, lifting him into the air and throwing him directly into the grill of a parked trash disposal unit.

He tumbled into a heap about five meters away from Jerry and Kat, and as he lay there, motionless, head twisted in an unnatural direction and neck bent sickeningly backwards, Jerry could see his left arm splayed out to the side, and on his wrist, gleaming in the harsh lights of the station concourse, an antique gold wristwatch.

4

THE WOMAN WAS GONE, of course.

But not before Jerry spied a sliver of her dress and a brief shimmer of brunette hair disappearing through the kitchen service door at the rear of the restaurant.

Outside, all was chaos. People were screaming, one woman fainted, blood was streaming from the dead man in a surprisingly strong flow, and the security guards were all running around in circles like a flock of chickens with their heads cut off. The adrenalin of the chase was still pumping through their veins and they didn't quite know how to exit from combat mode.

"Let me through, let me through, I'm a doctor," yelled a loud, commanding voice, and the crowd parted to let the man in. He bent down on one knee and turned his head to listen for sounds of breathing from the dead man's lips while he felt his neck, checking for a pulse.

After a moment, the man straightened up and said, to no one in particular, in a mildly sad, discouraged voice, "I'm sorry. It's no use. He's dead, Jim." And as he slowly moved away, melting back into the crowd, the people surged forward once again, craning their necks to get a good look at the gory scene, but not a single one of them seemed to notice that the man on the ground was no longer wearing a wristwatch.

"Just can't leave well-enough alone, can you, Jerry?" whispered Kat, as he sidled back up to her in the crush of people gathered at the restaurant door. "Don't think I didn't see what you did back there."

Jerry looked at her in wide-eyed innocence and said, "Who? Me? I just wanted to help out, that's all."

"Mmm hmm," said Kat, pursing her lips skeptically as Jerry waved over their waiter and laid a wad of banknotes on him before taking her hand and discreetly leading her away into the concourse.

As Jerry and Kat moved across the transitway and flagged down a passenger shuttle, a large, heavy-set man in a brown leather trench coat sitting beside a decorative fountain in the concourse rose to his feet, stepped to the edge of the transitway, and slipped into a waiting shuttle.

"DO YOU THINK, O Apple of My Eye, that maybe just once, just one single frikkin' time, we could have a simple vacation without you getting us involved in cloak-and-dagger shenanigans?" grumbled Kat as their shuttle zipped through the concourse towards their meet-up point.

"Hey, I didn't start anything here, Kat. That lady found *me*, remember?"

"And when she ran away you couldn't just let it go right there? You had to go and get us involved in yet another deadly game that's leading us God-knows-where?"

"Well, I grant you that I may have accelerated the pace of our involvement, but I have a feeling we were sunk no matter what we did – there's no doubt in my mind that someone will report that she sat with us in the restaurant, and eventually we'd be dragged into this mess. At least now we might be a little more in the driver's seat. I think that watch may be a key to this intrigue. We're better-off having it than not, if you ask me."

Kat sighed deeply. Mentally, she drew a thick red line through the word "Vacation" scrawled across her mind's calendar. She was probably paying for something horrible she'd done in a previous life. Maybe she'd been Genghis Khan's acupuncturist. Maybe without her assistance the Mongol hordes wouldn't have sacked half the ancient world if their leader had been stuck at home in bed with a bad back.

She sighed again. There were a lot of burned villages that demanded retribution. It was going to be a long winter.

WHEN JERRY AND KAT checked-in at their meetup point they were given two golden wristbands by a smiling attendant of indeterminate gender who flashed them a mouthful of startlingly-white perfectly smooth teeth while explaining, "These are VIP passes. Don't lose them. You'll need them for the return trip. You can use them to board any Elevator without having to make reservations."

"I don't want to be responsible for someone else getting booted from their spot just because I have some special pass," said Jerry hesitantly.

"Oh, there's no need to worry about that – every transport has a few places deliberately reserved for last-minute VIPs, like you two," said the attendant, flashing those pearly-whites at them again. "But you're in luck anyways – we've added a few extra Elevators to the schedule today, because of the festival and all. In fact, there's a descent leaving in forty-five minutes and only half the seats in first-class are taken. Most people prefer the overnight Elevators. Those offer a more leisurely descent with the opportunity to get a full night's sleep before arrival planetside. But if you prefer to take this one, you can wait for departure in our first-class lounge. The doors will open when they sense your passes."

"Do we need to clear security before boarding?"

"Oh no, there aren't any more security checkpoints. You won't be scanned again until you reenter this station, not even on the ground before ascent."

Jerry raised his eyebrows at this last statement. No checkpoints until they reentered the station? Which means that Management wasn't concerned about Elevator security, but mostly just interested in controlling station access. Curious.

Kat tugged Jerry forcefully towards the first-class lounge. "C'mon, Jer – let's get out of sight. I feel too exposed standing out here in the open."

As they disappeared into the lounge and the doors swished back shut behind them, a large heavy-set man in a dark brown leather trench coat approached the attendant and asked, "Excuse me, did I hear you say there are several first-class seats still available for the next Elevator?"

"Yes sir. Would you like me to reserve you a seat?"

"Yes, please. I need to be on that Elevator."

AS THEY SETTLED DOWN into comfy overstuffed leather armchairs in a quiet corner of the lounge, Jerry said, "I don't want to burst your bubble, Kat, but we're no less exposed here than we were in the open concourse." And with a flick of his eyes he indicated one of the ubiquitous security cameras mounted on the overhead bulkhead.

Kat directed a sad, sympathetic gaze at Jerry as she said softly, "Oh, Jerry, is that really all you think of me? I'm just a pretty face to you? Another empty-headed damsel in distress cowering behind your shield?" And she barked a short derisive snort at him.

"Well, Mr. Knight in Shining Armour, I hate to burst *your* bubble, but the moment that that Jezebel uttered the word 'danger' my Slimlines initiated a counter-surveillance protocol that I had the foresight to program a long time ago.

"Remember, once we cleared security after arrival, the station gave me access to their Travelers' Portal and their euphemistically named 'Welcome Center'. Which of course the station provides mainly to track and monitor all visitors onsite. But as soon as their system linked with my Slimlines, I was able to tunnel up through their primitive interface and access the station's mainframe. Their firewalls obviously weren't designed to withstand a stealth intrusion by a quantum computer.

"The *we're all in great danger* keyphrase automatically activated my security measures, which include altering all audio and video records of us in their system. Even right now, we can sit here and chat in full view of their surveillance system without worrying about prying eyes or ears."

"I'm not sure that's such a good thing, either, Kat. It's probably a red flag to anyone watching the system to see other people interacting with what looks like a blank space."

"I didn't say the Slimlines were erasing us from the video, Jerry – I said they were *altering* our images.

"Invariably, there are dead spots in any surveillance coverage. We walked for a half hour before you spotted that restaurant. At some point during that journey we passed through a small gap in the video coverage, and as far as the station's surveillance system is concerned, we never came back out.

"Instead, both in the recorded surveillance files and in the live feed, we now appear alternately as different looking people, sometimes two men, or two women, or maybe an adult and a child. Different people wearing different clothing each time we emerge from another surveillance gap in their coverage. Unless someone is specifically examining every moment of each camera's feed, it's highly unlikely anyone will notice the inconsistencies in the record, and any search for us will come up blank.

"But I can't do anything about in-person human observation. I don't know if anyone has been watching us since we left that restaurant, but if our description is already out there, I'd rather not stand around in public places on full display to every passerby."

Jerry smiled broadly and leaned over to plant a kiss on Kat's cheek.

"Don't sell yourself short, Kat. I never said you're just another pretty face. You've got a killer body, too."

His smile was replaced by a wince as Kat punched him forcefully in the arm.

"Ouch! And not a bad left jab, either."

AS THEY WERE USHERED onboard the Elevator, Kat and Jerry were handed a colourful brochure along with a booklet of instructions to be followed during the ride. They were then shown to a pair of comfortable seats in the first-class section, handed two drinking tubes of champagne and warm moist towelettes, and left to settle in for the journey.

"This is a strange affair, Jerry," said Kat, scanning the brochure. "According to this diagram, we're sitting in what looks like a huge teardrop vertically sliced in half that isn't even attached to the Elevator cable."

"That's right, Kat. This craft never actually makes physical contact with the cable – that would cause wear and tear. It's a lot like a maglev train – superconducting magnets use both attraction and repulsion to keep us close to the cable without drifting away, and at the same time provide acceleration and braking. The best thing is, the energy we create by braking the craft on the way down is fed back into the system to provide the energy to lift us back up on the return journey. It's quite elegant.

"The Elevator has to make room for the passage of other Elevators traveling in the other direction, so it's been designed in a half-moon shape, with the flat side facing the cable. And it tapers to a point at the end facing away from the planet to reduce aerodynamic resistance during the journey up through the atmosphere."

"And one thin cable can support all this?"

"That's the 'prohibitively expensive' part of the equation in making these things. The entire space station probably cost a mere fraction of what it cost to manufacture 60,000 kilometers of this cable."

"Did you just say '60,000 kilometers'? As in 40,000 miles?"

"Give or take, that's about right. Woven diamond nanothread coated with a flexible, 6-nanometer layer of hafnium diboride, an ultra-high-temperature ceramic with off-the-chart electrical conductivity. One meter of it costs more than our entire ship. I can't even begin to calculate the monetary amounts involved in the length we're talking about."

"Okay, I'm getting the gist of it, but one last question: why did they give us velcro slippers when we boarded?"

"So you can walk through the cabin during the first part of our descent – we start with one quick 2G burn for about 60 seconds and then we coast on our momentum for the next hour. That saves energy and reduces stress on the Elevator cable. But while we coast we'll feel weightless. The velcro slippers are designed to cling to the floor."

"Wouldn't magnetic boots be a better idea?"

"Uh-uh, Kat. There's actually a significant static magnetic field in this craft while the superconducting magnets are operational. It's not enough to pull the cutlery out of your hands, but it's strong enough to mess with the operation of magnetic-sensitive devices. That's why before boarding they ask each passenger if they have a pacemaker, and why you have to keep your Slimlines sealed in a copper-fiber pouch."

"So instead we'll just settle for being sterilized."

"No again – the magnetic flux density isn't high enough to significantly affect humans, despite all the so-called 'miracle' products that make questionable claims about the benefit of wearing magnets against your skin. There's some evidence to support the idea that it helps broken bones heal faster, and a few other limited applications, but no sterilization, I'm happy to report.

"But while we're in this vehicle: no computers, no phones, nothing with a chip or electronics of any kind."

"So we have to sit here for several hours with nothing to entertain us but" – *shudder* – "paper books and magazines."

Jerry's wide grin betrayed his delight.

"Yup. Welcome to *my* world, Kat. At least for the next few hours."

KAT WAS STRUGGLING with a pouch of beef bourguignon when the seal suddenly broke and sprayed a thick glop of sauce all over the front of her t-shirt. Cursing, she gave up and jammed the now-half-empty pouch back into the meal sack clipped to the tray table in front of her. She wiped off as much of the brown gravy as she could with a moist towelette but a thick coating remained. She brushed back for the thousandth time an errant strand of hair that lazily floated in front of her face and sighed in frustration.

"I'm not sure why they even try to feed us during this part of the descent – why don't they just wait until gravity returns when we start braking, so we can eat like normal human beings?"

Jerry looked up from the crossword puzzle he was filling in and smiled. He seemed perfectly at ease with their present situation, and had already finished his meal. He sipped leisurely from a small tube of scotch tethered to the drink holder.

"We can't eat during braking, Kat – the cabin crew won't be able to move around, and you certainly won't be able to do much more than lay painfully in your fully-reclined seat.

"The station offers slower scheduled departures, particularly the overnight trips, but this shuttle is the 'rapid'.

"Remember the 60-second burn when we took off? That was nothing. When we're ready to start braking, the Elevator reverses its vertical orientation and then this simulated zero-g will be replaced as the pressure rises to just over 3Gs. It'll be all you can do to keep breathing. Forget about lifting a fork to your mouth."

Kat looked at him with horror.

"And how long does *that* go on?"

"Oh, about 60 minutes, more or less. That's the longest most people can endure that pressure. It's the price we pay for a rapid descent. It's why the trip back up takes over eight times as long to complete, since the maximum climbing speed during the first half of the ascent never gets above 2,000 kilometers an hour at peak velocity. It picks up significantly once the Elevator clears the point of Geostationary Orbit, but climbing up from the planet is still a far sight slower than descending in free-fall."

"I'm starting to understand why tourism on this rock is so limited, Jer Bear."

"Just look at it as a good time to meditate. You know, discover your inner self."

"Jerry, if I have to endure 60 minutes of 3 Gs, I have a feeling most of the cabin will be discovering my "inner self" — toss me some of those handy paper bags they handed out at boarding. I might need our whole supply."

KAT NERVOUSLY WATCHED the overhead timer count down the minutes until the craft would initiate braking, and she chewed her lower lip in worry.

She glanced over at Jerry. He had fallen fast asleep and the now-empty little beverage tube bobbed in front of him on its tether. Jerry's crossword puzzle had escaped his grasp and undulated gently in the cabin's air currents. An attendant came by and snatched the paper from the air, then leaned over and retrieved the empty drink container.

The souvenir pencil Jerry had been using on his crossword puzzle did a slow-motion dance in front of Kat, peacefully twisting end over end like a tiny propeller on an invisible aircraft. *I rode the Wire!* was embossed in little gold letters on one side. Kat grabbed it out of the air and stuffed it into a side pocket on her cargo pants. It wouldn't be very pleasant for anyone to find *that* under their butt while they pressed down on it for 60 minutes. She winced at the thought.

Kat envied Jerry's complete unconcern at the ordeal they were about to undergo. Her own space experiences had always been in Langstrom-drive ships, where there was no inertia during travel. She had tolerated brief exposures to increased G-forces during the rare occasions that sub-lightspeed thrusters were utilized, but those instances had always been brief and fairly mild. 60 minutes at 3 Gs terrified her, and she contemplated the prospect with emotions bordering on hysteria.

When the cabin attendant gently touched her on her shoulder, Kat almost leaped out of her seat.

"Oh, I'm sorry, ma'am. I didn't mean to startle you."

"No, no – it's not you – I guess I'm just a little nervous, that's all. How can I help you?"

"Well, I'm just checking to see if you'd like to take this opportunity to put on your comfort garment, ma'am."

Kat eyed with distaste the adult diaper still sealed in its pouch and tucked into the storage pocket in front of her.

"Um, right…" said Kat, "I… I guess I haven't, ah, had a chance yet to slip that on…."

"Well, ma'am, I'm sorry to have to insist, but we do require it before the high-G portion of the trip commences. Think of it as a courtesy to the next passenger who will sit in this seat," added the attendant discreetly.

"If you would like to slip into one of the toilet facilities just to the rear, I see there are several with green lights. You should be able to make it back out with plenty of time to spare before braking commences."

Kat nodded in acquiescence, and unsteadily rose to her feet as the cabin attendant moved away. Carefully and deliberately placing each of her feet on the carpeting, she ponderously moved towards the back of the cabin. A sliding door hissed open at her approach and she moved into a small space boasting several narrow doors marked with little glowing lights.

Since most passengers had already changed, only a couple of doors displayed red lights. Kat moved to her right and pressed her hand against a green-lit door, which folded in at the middle and pulled aside to allow her to enter.

Sitting in a seat in the rearmost row of the first-class cabin, a large, heavy-set man in a dark brown leather trench coat watched Kat slip into the toilet facility. As the door closed behind her, he unclipped his seatbelt and rose to his feet, then turned and moved off in her direction.

**LANCING AT** the bathroom mirror, Kat grimaced to see the nasty brown stain all over the front of her t-shirt.

She quickly pulled it off, held it under the sink faucet and turned on the water. Instantly, her shirt was almost ripped out of her hands by the powerful suction from the sink drain. *Oh, right. Zero-G.* The suction would draw the water into the drain. *Clever design.*

She vigourously rubbed at the dried gravy under the spray from the faucet, then carefully wrung out her shirt and turned off the water, killing the drain suction. She didn't pull her shirt back on immediately but let it drift away, hoping it might dry out a bit floating in the warm air.

Now for the Main Event. She sighed in annoyance.

Kat cursed quietly as she struggled with removing her pants. The bulky legs of the cargo pants had been a comfortable choice to travel in, but in zero-g they were just annoying, wrapping around her ankles as she struggled to pull them off each leg while keeping one foot wedged into a slipper that clung to the flooring.

She was about to step out of them so she could remove her underwear when the door to the toilet cubicle exploded inwards, ramming into her butt and smashing her face against the wall.

Nose bleeding profusely and her head spinning, Kat blinked in confusion, trying to understand what had just happened. The door had once again slid shut and a very large man was reaching for her neck as Kat tried to turn and get her bearings.

The impact had knocked her out of the single slipper she had been wearing, and trying to straighten up sent her bobbing upwards to the overhead bulkhead.

Her attacker missed her neck and only managed to grab her shoulder to forcefully pull her back down, which sent him on his own upwards trajectory as the tiny velcro slippers on his huge feet weren't up to the task of anchoring him to the carpeting. He was taller than Kat, and his momentum smacked his head into the overhead bulkhead, but it didn't seem to bother him at all.

The force of his tug on her shoulder had brought Kat back down to the floor, and she tried to spin around to face the man, but was tripped-up by her pants, which were still bundled around her ankles, preventing her from separating her feet by more than a few inches.

Struggling to navigate this murderous see-saw game, Kat saw her assailant returning downwards, thrusting out his fist at her face.But he managed only to punch her in her shoulder, with the force of his motion sending him spinning backwards and against the toilet as he flailed sideways.

Seizing the opportunity, Kat brought both fists down onto the side of his neck, hoping to smash his face against the counter as he drifted over it. Her blow was weakened, though, as her downward motion was thwarted by the inverse force that lifted her body up off the floor.

It gave the man the chance he needed to grab Kat by the wrist with an iron grip and haul her toward him.

Taking advantage of the momentary stabilization that her attacker's grip provided, Kat spun herself around to face him, wrapping her imprisoned arm against her sternum as she brought her elbow down as forcefully as she could against the man's face. She was rewarded with the sound of a satisfying crunch as the cartilage in his nose collapsed beneath her elbow.

Again, though, he displayed absolutely no reaction to the blow. Still clenching her wrist in his crushing paw, he brought his other arm up viciously and smashed his fist directly into the side of her head.

It was like being hit with a 20-lb sledgehammer. Kat's head snapped to the side. Her vision clouded over as her legs turned to rubber.

Grunting with satisfaction, the man wrapped his arm around her neck as her own arm relaxed and she began to drift away. He squeezed his forearm against her windpipe and began choking her, forming a vicelike grip by wrapping his other fist around his wrist and pulling tight.

Kat knew from her jujitsu training that she needed to bend forward and down to break his grip, but because they were grappling in zero-g, her movement had no effect on her position, and the pressure he was applying to her throat only increased.

Frantically, Kat straightened up and arched her back against him, then reached up and clawed blindly at his face. A short curse of pain escaped the man's lips as one of her fingernails scraped his eyeball. He relaxed his grip only briefly, but it was all Kat needed to grab his arm with both hands and pull it off her throat.

She spun away from him, but she still lacked the space to get off a kick or a straight-arm jab to his throat. He then wrapped both his meaty hands around her neck and pressed his thumbs hard against her windpipe.

Kat found herself unable to draw a breath and frantically kicked out against the man, bringing her knees up and pushing them against his chest, trying to force herself away from him.

It was like trying to push a wall. Her attacker just grinned and pulled Kat closer to him. She could feel his breath puffing out against her and he stared into her eyes while squeezing his thumbs firmly against her throat. Slowly, their bodies rotated in unison in the air, locked together by the crushing grip of his fingers on her neck.

Kat smacked at his face with both hands and pummeled his head on both sides but he just laughed. It was as though he were being swatted by a kitten.

As her field of vision narrowed, Kat lowered her eyes and saw her cargo pants, still bunched up around her calves beneath her knees that were firmly wedged against the man's chest. She spotted something peeking out from the side pocket on one leg, and she stopped pounding the man on his head just long enough to reach down and pull the pencil out of her pants pocket. Gripping it as tightly as she could, she swung her arm out and then brought it back hard, ramming the pencil into his ear and several inches deep into his head.

His grip on Kat's throat immediately relaxed, and his eyes went blank. As his arms fell limp, her legs straightened and sent the man crashing backward into the opposite wall.

Still gasping heavily from her near asphyxiation, she cautiously pushed herself over to where he floated at the other side of the cubicle. Kat knew all about the resilience of the human body and wasn't confident she'd actually killed him. She'd read about people surviving worse injuries.

Grasping him by his ankles, she pulled him horizontal and spun him face up. When the angle was just right, she pushed him downward until the back of his neck was resting on the edge of the toilet bowl.

She reached down and activated the fans to start a powerful suction in the bowl. Normally, just as in the sink, the fans suck down any material near the bowl. They worked nicely to keep the man's head in place while Kat gritted her teeth and wrenched the pencil back out from his ear canal. She curled her lip in disgust as blood and shreds of brain dripped off the little spike and were sucked away.

Positioning the pencil against his left eye, she held it upright and slammed the heel of her hand down onto it. With a popping-gooshing sound it plunged down through his eyeball and disappeared into his head. Only the stub of the eraser remained visible, protruding from the bloody eyeball like a cartoon exclamation mark.

Floating up and off to the side, Kat reached down and finally pulled her cargo pants up to her waist, cinching them closed. She pushed herself down to the floor and slipped her feet into her slippers, then spotted the diaper, still dreamily bobbing around in the cubicle. *Maybe another time,* she thought, and stuffed it down into her pants pocket.

She looked into the mirror and studied herself. She was a horror show. Her hair floated in disarray like a fright wig, and blood from her nosebleed was smeared all over her face and down her chest.

She pulled a length of toilet paper from the holder, wet it under the faucet, then wiped as much blood as she could off her face and chest. Little droplets of blood swirled in the air but were gradually heading towards the toilet, where the fans still whirred.

She pushed the wad of blood-soaked paper down into the bowl where it was promptly sucked away. Finally, she pulled on her t-shirt and gathered her hair back into a rough approximation of a ponytail.

Examining herself in the mirror, she was relieved she had worn black today – any tiny droplets of blood on her shirt or pants might not be readily visible. Calmly, she slid the door open and slipped into the corridor, sliding the door shut behind her.

Almost simultaneously, klaxons started wailing throughout the Elevator. Kat saw all the lights on the toilet cubicle doors switch to red as the doors automatically locked shut for the remainder of the journey.

Hustling back to her seat, Kat had barely enough time to get seated and strap herself in before the countdown timer started flashing red as the numbers hit the 30-second warning.

"I was wondering how long you were going to take before coming back," said Jerry, who was now awake and looking at her with some concern. "You pushed it to the last minute. You sure like to live dangerously, Kat."

IN PREPARATION FOR the high-G deceleration, the Elevator passenger compartments began a slow vertical 180° rotation on internal swivel mounts.

While they were waiting for the rotation to complete and the compartments to lock into position, Jerry turned to Kat and said, "I changed on the station so I haven't had a chance to check out the toilets here. Are they nice?"

Kat looked at him sideways and said, "Well, the one I used was clean enough but I wouldn't want to go in there now. I really destroyed it."

6

NCE THEY WERE on the ground and waiting to pick up their luggage before entering the ground station concourse, Kat brought Jerry up to speed on her assault in the toilet cubicle. Jerry was predictably horrified.

"Why didn't you tell me sooner, Kat?!"

"Why, Jerry? What would you have done? Gone inside to search him and gotten caught with a dead body? That's *exactly* why I didn't let you know about it."

"Well, did you at least go through his pockets?"

"To tell the truth, Jer, I had other things on my mind, like getting out of there before some helpful attendant came by to check up on me.

"Besides, I think we both know what he was after. His wallet and house keys probably wouldn't tell us much we need to know."

"I suppose your concern about direct in-person surveillance was on the mark, Kat. And he probably took a picture of us at some point."

"Which means our image is in their system. My program will still block any facial recognition processes from tagging us, but that won't stop them from sending out any photos he snapped."

"You know, Kat, I'm not sure this assassin was working for the space station – this feels like a private contractor to me. If the station wanted to grab us, all they had to do was to wait until the Elevator landed and simply detain us then.

"I think this guy might be part of a completely different vector of danger."

Kat rolled her eyes skyward.

"Well that's just great. It's becoming a real party now."

"Look at the bright side – they probably don't have anywhere near the resources the station has, which puts us on much more of an even footing with them."

"Here's our bags, Jer – let's get out of this place."

Kat grabbed their suitcases but Jerry held her arm before she could move away. "Hold on, Kat. We don't want to walk out there along with the rest of the passengers. No doubt there's more of our new friends waiting for us. They'll be pretty disappointed to see us instead of their buddy."

"So what do we do, then? We can't bed down in here for the rest of the trip."

"I see an access door over there for service personnel, which should work out perfectly. My contact is onsite, and that's probably the most efficient way to get to him. Plus, it helps us disappear from the mass of arriving passengers."

Just at that moment, a loud shout came from the direction of the Elevator access ramp, and some sort of commotion seemed to roil the remaining stream of passengers slowly disembarking the craft.

"Looks like your handiwork has been discovered, Kat. Thank the stars for first-class priority exit protocols. I'm glad not to be stuck back there now. Let's get going."

As discreetly as they could, they sidled casually over to the service access door. Kat made a tiny movement with her jaw and the little light on the keypad switched to green, releasing the door latch with a loud click. They slipped into the corridor on the other side.

They found themselves in a wide, harshly lit passageway that stretched as far as the eye could see. People were hustling along in both directions, pushing carts, peering at tablets, carrying tools, or plodding along with tired expressions on their faces. Little ID badges were clipped to shirt pockets or hanging from lanyards around their necks.

Kat's Slimlines mapped out a route for them to Engineering. They tried to look like they belonged but within a few minutes their luggage caught the attention of one of the passersby.

"Are you folks lost? This area is only for station personnel."

"No, no, we're good," replied Jerry quickly. "We were actually sent this way – we're on our way to Engineering. A friend of our works there and he asked us to come by."

The man frowned and said, "Hm. They really should have given you Visitor Badges." He rolled his eyes skyward. "Well, I can't say it's the first time they've ignored protocol. Who are you here to see?"

"Slaäm Latching. Head of Engineering, I believe."

"Chief Latching?" said the man happily, and a broad smile appeared on his face. "No problem – I can take you right to him. The Chief's a great guy – any friend of his is a friend of mine. My name's Wilkins. I'm actually his Second in Command. I'm pleased to meet you." He stuck out his hand and gave them each a hearty handshake.

As Wilkins led them deeper and deeper into the bowels of the ground station, Kat kept track of their progress on her Slimlines. Predictably, Engineering was buried on the lowest level at almost the exact center of the facility.

The amount of machinery required to keep the station running was overwhelming. As they entered the main Engineering section, walls became covered with panels of blinking lights, data readouts and graphical displays. People with thoughtful looks on their faces moved about or sat hunched over at workstations, methodically tapping away.

They came up to a glass-walled space and their guide indicated the open door.

"There you go, folks. I'll leave you here. It was nice meeting you."

Jerry tapped a knuckle on the open door and said, "Slaäm? Got time for an old friend?"

The man behind the desk was sitting with his back to them as he studied a readout of several columns of data scrolling across a large wall panel. He looked to be in his late thirties and sported a slight middle-age spread that left his stomach bulging out slightly above his belt. He had close-cropped sandy hair and a short matching beard that barely concealed his jawline. He was wearing a long-sleeve pale blue shirt but had rolled up both sleeves to his elbows. A faded military tattoo was still barely visible on his left forearm.

At the sound of Jerry's voice he spun around and exclaimed, "Jerry! You made it! And this must be Kat! You didn't lie – she's gorgeous! Great to see both of you – come in!"

"Wow. Such a warm welcome," said Kat

"Well I haven't seen Jerry in almost a decade – one of my favourite people, don't you know. We used to stay up well into the wee hours drinking and telling lies. I sure do miss those days."

"I miss them, too, Slaäm. But I don't miss the work. Looks like you've done okay for yourself here, though."

"This little gig? Oh sure, it pays the bills, I suppose."

"Don't be modest – sounds like you're a real big wheel around here."

"Sure, in the ass-end of the galaxy, on a medieval planet stuck in the stone ages. A dream job if that's what turns you on."

"This doesn't look all that medieval to me," said Kat quietly, glancing over at the equipment and data displays filling the room outside.

"That's because you haven't seen the actual planet yet."

Turning to Jerry, he said, "I don't want to be a bad host but your timing really couldn't be worse – there's some kind of hullabaloo going on upstairs. Something about the last Elevator that just arrived. Say – that was your ride, right?"

"Ah, yeah, I think so…."

"Well, apparently something crazy happened on board and all department heads are being called to Central Control for an emergency meeting. I pray to God it's not an Engineering issue – I've already got enough on my plate."

"Yeah, no problem, Slaäm – Kat and I can meet up with you later – maybe catch up over drinks tonight? I doubt this problem will involve you. I didn't notice any operational issues on the trip. It's probably not an Engineering matter."

"From your lips to God's ears, Jer. And drinks sounds just great. I'll give you directions to an excellent hotel and we can meet in their bar tonight around eight."

"Perfect," said Jerry.

"Let me get you a couple of Courtesy Badges so you can move around the station easily," he said, riffling around in a drawer in his desk, then finally extracting a pair of bright red cards dangling from two red lanyards.

"These are all-access – a perk from being with Engineering – we can go anywhere, of course. They'll open any door on the station.

"Now, you probably want to change before heading out to the village – or are you going to buy some duds upstairs?"

"Um, no, I figured I'd take care of all that at the hotel?..." replied Jerry, puzzled.

Slaäm raised his eyebrows and said, "Well, that's up to you. Pretty brave of you, though. Not sure I'd have the guts to try it myself, but whatever cranks your rotor, right?"

"Yeah…."

"So you two took the high-G trip. And this was probably your first Elevator ride," said Slaäm to Kat, as he walked them back out to the main corridor. "How did you like it?"

Kat looked at him sideways.

"It was murder."

7

KAT AND JERRY wanted to exit the Elevator facility as discreetly as possible, and that meant avoiding the public area of the station at all costs.

Kat searched for available exits on her Slimlines and identified an employee/vendor access gate far off to the side from the main gate. Happily, it opened right onto the main road leading to the village. All they'd have to do is slip through onto the street and blend in with all the other travelers coming from the station.

"Turn left here, Jerry," said Kat, eyes flickering behind her Slimlines. "This corridor will feed us directly into the transitway going to the vendor gate."

"I feel like I'm wandering through the tunnels beneath Disneyland," he replied, peering down the myriad passageways that stretched off to either side as they made their way along. "This place must go for miles."

"And everything's cryptically marked, with notations like 'E28SB11'," she said, looking up at the wall markings as they passed another intersection.

"If I had to guess, I imagine that would mean 'East 28, Sub-Basement 11', or some such code."

"Thank God for my glasses. Even Theseus would be hard-pressed to find his way out of this place."

"Let's hope we don't meet up with any horned monsters in the meantime," chuckled Jerry, but the thought just made Kat shudder.

"Not funny, Jer. Not after the day I've had."

"Oh, lighten up, Kat. We're on vacation, remember?"

And guffawing heartily, he strode ahead, his laugh echoing eerily through the empty corridors.

THE CORRIDOR TERMINATED at a bank of freight elevators. Jerry and Kat rode one up to the surface level, where an area of loading docks and access doors let them exit into the open air. Outside, an enormous staging area was bounded by a service road coming from a gate in a tall security wall that stretched away out of sight.

The weather was warm, but heavily overcast, and a steady drizzle misted the air around them.

"Oh, wonderful," said Kat, annoyed at the prospect of arriving at the hotel soaked to the bone. "I don't think I packed any foul-weather gear. This must be what your friend was talking about when he suggested we pick up some new clothes in the station."

"Well, at least it's not cold out. The Elevator is situated dead-smack on the planet's equator. Just grin and bear it — we'll catch a cab and be soaking in a hot bath at the hotel before you know it."

They hadn't gone more than ten meters from the station when Kat noticed a small red light in the corner of her glasses. Tapping her teeth together, she said, "Report."

"I'm sorry, Kat," came the soft response in her ear canal, "But I've just lost all network connections."

"Can you access our ship?"

"Sorry, I can't access anything. There are no carrier signals anywhere in range."

Kat looked at Jerry with concern.

"There's no network coverage here, Jer. None at all. No phone, web, or any other service. It's a complete dead zone."

"I understand the whole planet's like that, Kat. I read they even made the ground station install special shielding so none of its coverage could leak out."

"But Jer, I've never been anywhere there wasn't *some* kind of coverage – not even when we were on safari in the middle of nowhere on Africanus Majoris."

"Well, not here, babe. In fact, you'd better pray no one twigs that those glasses are more than just lenses to help you see better – computer possession can get you booted off-planet in a heartbeat, and they'll probably want to confiscate and destroy them, too."

"Jerry! *WHY* did we come here?"

"Don't panic, babe. Just be cool, and we'll be fine. With any luck we'll blend in perfectly with all the other offworlders and be back on our way in three days with no one the wiser."

Grumbling and cursing under her breath, Kat followed Jerry up to the gate. A security guard in a little booth took one look at their red badges and the gate swung open for them.

They stepped into the street outside the gate and promptly sank ankle-deep into mud. There was mud everywhere. The road was mud, the walkway beside it was mud, the people were splashed with mud, the wagons and horses were covered in mud—

"Wait." said Kat. "Horses? Wagons? Dirt road? What in the world is going on here?"

The road was busy with traffic heading to and fro past the ground station. But there wasn't a car or truck in sight.

Most people were plodding along on foot through the muck and manure that covered the roadway. Their clothing seemed to consist mostly of heavy woolen cloaks or shawls draped over layers of damp linen. Everyone wore knee-high boots laced up to the top with leather straps.

The roadway was peppered with makeshift wooden stalls and various merchants hawking all manner of goods. Kat could see the station's main gate about a mile down the road, where an especially thick cluster of stalls almost completely clogged the road on both sides.

A slow line of teetering wagons pulled by drayhorses wended their way through the melee, driven by tired-looking men dressed in dirty work clothes.

Kat turned to Jerry. "What. The. F—" but before she could complete her thought, she staggered backwards as a huge glop of mud sailed through the air and smacked into her face.

A dirty-faced boy of about 11 years stood ten feet away and crowed triumphantly at her, yelling, "Yaa! Dirty pagans! Devils' wear! A pox on you!"

As he yelled, several other children nearby joined in, calling out various pejoratives and flinging handfuls of mud and pebbles at Jerry and Kat, who staggered back under the onslaught.

"Here! Stop it, you little demons!" yelled out a woman, who rushed at the children, swinging a long stick in front of her and smacking a couple of them on their butts as they ran away.

She turned and looked at Kat and said, "Oh, I'm so sorry my dear, those little urchins are nothing but trouble. But you shouldn't be here dressed like that, you know, you'll just egg them on. Was your tourney gear stolen?"

"Um, yes," answered Jerry. "And we haven't had a chance to find any others…. We've had a strange day."

The woman looked at Jerry with no small measure of disapproval, then said, "Well, you shouldn't be so careless. Mud in your face is the least you can expect if you come out dressed like that. You'll never make it to the village in one piece wearing those clothes."

"What are we going to do then?" asked Kat, clawing the mud from her hair and scraping a glop of it off her face. "We don't have any others with us."

"Leave it to me, dear," she said, smiling sympathetically at Kat and then glancing over at Jerry to shoot him the evil eye again. "Wait here for just a moment."

The woman splashed through the mud over to a wagon a few meters away.

"Hoy! Elric! A moment, if you would. I have a small boon to ask of thee. I would hire your wagon, kind sir."

"Alas, Matilde, my load is already all my dray can bear."

Craning up on her toes to speak to the man, the woman lowered her voice and said, "Not even for offworld credits from two rich tourists?"

The man's eyes widened in surprise and said, "Well, that tells a different story. Where might I find such an unexpected blessing?"

Jerking her shoulder in Jerry and Kat's direction, the woman said, "Right there, but we can't waste time jawboning about it. Time is of the essence." And indeed, already a small crowd was starting to collect near Kat and Jerry, with discontented grumbling leaking out.

Gesturing to Kat, the woman indicated they should come over to the wagon. Stumbling through the mud, pulling their soiled luggage after them, they staggered over to the wagon where she said quietly, "Get into the back of the wagon and lie down. Pull the canvas covering far enough over you to hide your clothes. Elric will take you where you need to go. Lie there quietly until you reach your lodgings."

As Kat and Jerry scrambled up onto the wagon and slipped under the canvas tarp, the woman turned to the small group of people who still milled about and hollered, "Well, what are you all looking at? Have you never seen offworlders before? On about your business, you lot, before I put a hex on all of you!"

Then she hoisted herself up onto the bench beside the wagon driver and said contentedly, "And I may as well get a ride out of this, too. I've had enough of this mud to last me a lifetime." And the wagon started back up on its bouncy, shaky path down the mud-covered road.

A half-hour of jostling later, something was crawling on Kat's skin under her t-shirt and she scratched frantically, trying to eject the creature before it could find a permanent home.

She and Jerry were laying on an assemblage of farm products. A sack near her left foot felt suspiciously like a collection of various meaty parts from a large animal, and two large bags of grain closer to her head sagged precariously on a stack of kindling, threatening to tumble off and down onto her.

The bales of hay they were laying on had at first appeared to be a pleasant option, but it soon became apparent that hay is neither soft nor comfortable, and little bits stuck into them like needles. Meanwhile, several species of tiny insects emerged from the bales to explore the unexpected treat of two warm bodies appearing like a gift from insect heaven.

"Ouch! Jerry, something's making a meal out of me! Several somethings, I think. If we stay here much longer we'll be whittled-down to our skeletons!"

"Patience, Kat. Let me check on our progress."

"Ah, excuse me, my good man," he called out, in what he hoped was an obsequious tone, "Is the hotel much farther?"

"Your Inn is within a few minutes travel, young one," replied the voice. "

"Oh, thank God," groaned Jerry.

"We'll not be taking the Name of the Creator in vain in this town, young sir!" came back Matilde's voice in a harsh rebuke. "We're all good God-fearing Christians here and you'd best be remembering that!"

"I wonder if that includes the mud-slinging residents, too," muttered Kat under her breath. Jerry gave her a small kick.

"So Jerry," she whispered, "I've been meaning to ask: how's that 'blending in with the other tourists' thing working out for you?"

Jerry sighed and pulled the canvas tarp higher up over his face.

Eventually the wagon's movement slowed and came to a stop near the door of a noisy establishment illuminated with several kerosene lanterns hanging from the entrance awning.

A large wooden sign swung gently in the breeze, hanging from a horizontal pole sticking out of the pub wall. A picture on the placard depicted a large brown cat sitting hunched over and apparently spitting out an indistinct chunk of matter.

"Here we are," said Elric. "The *Coughing Cat Arms*."

Kat timidly peeked out from the canvas tarp, and seeing no passersby, leapt up and batted at her shirt and pants, hoping to dislodge most of the hitchhikers beneath them.

Jerry threw their bags onto the ground then helped her down.

"We owe you our lives, my friends," said Jerry gratefully. "Apparently, we wouldn't have survived the trip out here on our own."

"Not dressed like that, you wouldn't have," said Matilde. "I advise you to find some proper garments before you tread the streets again, young one."

As for payment, Elric sheepishly asked Jerry for five offworld credits, but it was apparent this was only an opening bid, and he was prepared to drop his price substantially. Jerry was dumbfounded, and told him that he wouldn't permit him to take less than twenty credits, which almost set the fellow to weeping.

Jerry forced Matilde to take twenty credits, too, for her help, and when both of them protested that this was far too much to accept, what with them being good Christians and opposed to taking advantage of others, Jerry merely instructed them to give to the Church whatever they thought was excessive. That calmed them down somewhat, and the argument was over.

Before they left though, Matilde pressed a small wooden token into Kat's hand and whispered, "That's my mark. If you need help for any reason while you're here, come seek me out. Show that to anyone and they'll know how to find me."

Kat gave her a hug and she and Jerry waved goodbye, then pulled open the door and walked inside the Inn.

**ERRY AND KAT** stepped into a dark and noisy room, filled with crowded tables of men and women carousing and shouting to be heard over music coming from a spirited troupe of musicians.

The entrance foyer they stepped into was the best-lit place in the room, and not by accident – it allowed the assembled patrons to get a good look at any new arrivals before the entrants' eyes could properly adjust to the dimly lit room.

Their entrance was met with a hush in the various conversations around the room, and a few mumbled words of discontent.

Jerry felt a grip on his arm as the Innkeeper, always alert to any potentially furniture-damaging events, pulled him aside.

"Come here, you two," he said, leading them to an alcove with a small stand-up desk and lamp.

"I assume you're here to check in. What name is your reservation?"

"Um, no reservation. We didn't know we needed one."

"On Tourney Weekend?" the hotelier asked in a surprised tone. "Well, as luck would have it, we actually *do* have a suite available – we just got a last-minute cancellation. Apparently there was some sort of a problem on one of the Elevators and

the station has suspended all remaining transports for the day until they can sort it out. The party who reserved this suite is stuck in orbit until tomorrow, at the earliest. It's too bad — they'll miss the Opening Ceremonies.

"But their bad luck is your good fortune, I suppose. The Good Lord is smiling on you today, I think."

"And every day," added Jerry piously.

"Amen to that, Milord," said the innkeeper solemnly.

While Jerry was checking-in and filling out paperwork, Kat wandered back to the main entrance and discreetly peeked out into the pub. Immediately, a large glop of mashed potatoes flew through the air and impacted with her left eye.

"Son of a —" she swore, and staggered back to the alcove, where she stood grumbling beside Jerry and wiping potato off her face.

The Innkeeper couldn't help but chuckle quietly.

"I wouldn't try going back out there until you've had a chance to change, Milady. This crowd doesn't tolerate heretics any too kindly, I'm afraid."

"Change into what?" asked Kat peevishly. "We don't have anything but more clothes like these."

"You came to Tourney expecting to wear *that?*"

"Ah, no no," interrupted Jerry. "Our other luggage was stolen. Our tourney outfits were in there."

"Well then, you're doubly-blessed today, Milord. Our couturier is still open and you have just enough time to pick up a few outfits that should see you through the weekend."

Just at that moment the Innkeeper noticed the watch on Jerry's wrist and he visibly paled.

"Saints above! You need to remove that immediately, my friend! You'll be drawn and quartered if anyone spots that!" and he gently took the quill from Jerry's hand to allow him to unstrap his watch and drop it into his pants pocket.

The hotelier was visibly sweating now, and with a measure of relief he gently ushered Jerry and Kat away from the pub room and into a small shop filled with various garments.

"Estrilda, these two guests need full outfits for the next three days. Take care of them, won't you please?" And bowing his head, he nervously slipped back toward the check-in desk.

A plump, pleasant-looking woman bustled over to them, but her delight at hearing this unexpected good news noticeably dimmed when she caught sight of Kat's face, bruised, slightly bloodied, with mud and mashed potatoes squashed into her hair, and she actually tsk-tsk'ed.

"Leofric, come here, would you? I need you to attend to this squire whilst I tend to this lass. Come with me, dear. We'll need to clean you up a bit before we set to dressing you."

Sitting Kat down in a small alcove at the back of the shop, she began brushing out Kat's hair and pulling out the tangles.

"Egad, youngling, whatever have you been into? And are those bruises on your neck?"

"Yeah, about that…."

"You haven't been up to any mischief, have you?" asked Estrilda in a slightly reproachful tone.

"No, just a small wrestling match with a tree…."

"With a tr—? Oh, nevermind. We'll get you all fixed up right away, Good Lord willing, and no more waggery for you!"

"As God is my witness, I'll do my best, Estrilda, but I don't want to make any promises I can't keep."

The woman just clucked her tongue disapprovingly, then continued pulling at the knots in Kat's ruined hair.

Within a half-hour Kat and Jerry had been measured from head to toe and everywhere else, and fitted with at least a dozen outfits each. Estrilda let them go upstairs to their room to wash up while she put their purchases together, promising to send everything up promptly once she'd calculated the bill.

Leofric led them up a rear stairway to their room so they wouldn't have to brave the pub room again, and Kat gratefully flopped down on the bed as soon as the door closed behind them.

"Ohhhh, Jerry, what a day I've had! Pleeeeeease tell me there's a proper bathtub in that bathroom. If you say there's just a ceramic bowl and a pitcher of lukewarm water, I swear I'll end it all right now."

"No, I'm sorry to break your streak, Kat, but it appears the Universe has decided to take pity on you. There's a full-sized tub here. Actually, one that looks even big enough for two… and… hold on a moment… yes! Hot water. Real glorious hot water!

"And bubble bath beads!

"And candles!"

Jerry—" came Kat's voice from the bedroom. "Jerry, you need to stop there. If the next word out of your mouth is 'champagne', I'll pass out from sheer ecstasy."

"Can't hear you, Kat – I'm getting out of these wet clothes and into the tub. Come join me when your strength returns."

Groaning, Kat staggered to her feet and turned in the direction of the bathroom, when she heard a quiet knock at the door. Cursing, she stumbled over and yanked it open, only to come face-to-face with a large, heavy-set man wearing a long brown leather trench coat.

9

AT LEAPT BACK in terror from the door, spinning away and flinging herself across the room. Frantically, her eyes searched for anything sharp or heavy that she could grab, but she spotted nothing nearby.

Leaping up onto the bed, she set her feet in the best jujitsu defensive stance she could think of, and snarled at the man, "Think twice, bozo! Unless you've got a machete underneath that coat, you're in for a real beating if you come even one step closer."

The man at the door didn't move, but his expression was one of bewilderment.

"Beg pardon, Milady? My mistress hath bidden me to deliver thee thy garments. I cry thy mercy if I have offendeth thee." And he reached down to his side and picked up several large packages wrapped in paper. Stepping tentatively into the room, all the while keeping a wary eye on Kat, he carefully laid the packages on a wide ottoman beside a coffee table.

Cautiously backing out of the room, he tugged briefly on his eyebrow and said, "I shall leave thee now, Milady. Prithee forgive my intrusion. I bid thee good night." He closed the door then quickly thudded away down the hallway.

Stepping into the bathroom, Kat staggered over to the tub and sat down hard on the edge. Jerry was right – it was a huge tub, and he sat contentedly at one end covered in a generous layer of soap bubbles.

"Kat? Are you okay, babe? You're pale as a sheet. You need to take it easy, hon – I think all this travel is getting to you."

Kat just looked at Jerry with a glassy-eyed expression and mumbled incoherently under her breath. Moving like a dazed zombie, she pulled off her muddy clothes and dropped them onto the floor, stepped into the tub, then slowly slid down and disappeared beneath the surface of the water.

A LONG NAP was what they both needed, and after their bath they collapsed on the bed and promptly passed out. Kat's Slimlines buzzed her awake when the local time hit 7:30 and she prodded Jerry in the ribs with an elbow.

"Up and at 'em, babe. We have a dinner date, remember?"

"Ohhhhhhh, just give me five minutes more, Kat…."

"Uh-uh, bub. You're getting up *now!*" And with a forceful shove she rolled Jerry off the bed and onto the floor, then sat giggling while he cursed and scrambled to his feet.

"It's going to take time to get dressed, Jerry. We've got to navigate through these new garments they brought us. I think the evening wear are those, on the top."

It was complicated figuring out all the ties, straps and various bindings, but eventually they were both properly attired and looking like they'd stepped right out of Chaucer's Canterbury Tales.

"I like your little skirt and stockings, Jer," said Kat, giggling.

"It's called a 'kirtle', Kat – at least, that's what Leofric told me. And given the choice between wearing this and a long robe that sweeps the ground, I'll settle for this any day. And the silk tunic is actually quite comfortable. Not bad at all."

He moved over to the mirror to admire himself, twisting back and forth to take in the full effect.

When he was satisfied with what he saw in the mirror, Jerry turned around, took one look at Kat's bodice and smiled broadly, saying, "Now that alone makes the whole ordeal worthwhile!"

Kat grimaced and looked down at her cleavage spilling over the top of her tightly-laced low-cut gown.

"This is disgusting. I feel on display."

"Just be glad this is medieval England and not France – in the French Court at this time it was all the rage to wear your gown open at the top without covering your breasts at all. Imagine how you'd feel about *that*."

"I'd feel lonely, that's how, because I'd be sitting at home while you went out galivanting all by yourself. As it is, I'm already thinking twice about going out in public dressed in this obscene torture device."

"Then you're going to love it tomorrow, when we go to the Tourney. As I understand it, you need to apply makeup to your nipples so they can be clearly seen through your lace top."

"Oh no, that's not gonna happen. You're just dreaming, now, buddy."

"Just as well, Kat," said Jerry, leaning over and planting a wet kiss on her lips. "If you did that I doubt I'd be able to pay much attention to the games in the arena.

"And now, let's get going, hon – I believe the time has come."

THE PUB ROOM was hopping when they walked in, and this time no one took any notice of them as they wound their way through the crowd over to a table at the far side where Slaäm was already seated, clutching a huge tankard of golden liquid. He was dressed in a peasant's outfit, with a tattered day coat over a faded blue tunic. He blended in perfectly with the crowd of regulars filling the room.

A buxom barmaid with arms like a stevedore's barreled past them carrying a tray loaded down with several frothy tankards. Kat sidestepped a drunken reveler and plopped down into an empty chair opposite Slaäm. Jerry stood back a moment, frowning at the tableau.

"What's the matter hon?" asked Kat.

"Um, well, I don't really want to sit with my back to the door – would one of you like to swap places with me?"

Slaäm laughed heartily and Kat rolled her eyes, then stood up and moved over to the empty chair next to Slaäm.

"We're not in the Wild West, here, Jerry," said Slaäm. "I think you can relax a bit."

Kat and Jerry exchanged skeptical glances, then shrugged.

"Maybe you're right, Slaäm," said Jerry as he lowered himself into his chair. "After all, we *are* on vacation," which prompted Kat to shoot him a look that said, *Don't go there, buddy.*

"You two look great, now that you've changed into proper garb."

"Yeah, about that, Slaäm," said Jerry, "I would've appreciated a bit of heads-up on the situation – Kat and I were almost tarred and feathered on our way over here. If we hadn't been rescued by a kindly soul on the road we'd probably be hanging from the rafters in some barn right now."

"Well, I *did* mention that you needed to change, Jer. But I figured that station security, at least, would have stopped you from leaving dressed as you were – they're supposed to keep the tourists from putting themselves in danger like that. I'm surprised you made it off the property without being turned back."

"We didn't leave by the main gate – we took the service access gate on the east side."

Slaäm raised his eyebrows slightly and said, "Now why would you want to do that?" and then added, "And the gate guard there didn't stop you?"

"Once we flashed our red badges at him he just opened the gate without a word. You were right – those are real 'no questions asked' passes."

"Hm. He still should have cautioned you…. Oh well, you're here now and none the worse for wear, apparently. How do you like it so far?"

"Honestly," said Kat, "I wasn't expecting the whole Renaissance Faire experience. That sort of caught me by surprise."

"What else were you expecting when you came to a planet called 'Camelot'? Musical theatre?"

"I dunno… maybe some quaint English villages with swans and bed & breakfasts?"

"So I take it you didn't read the packet of instructions you got when boarding the Elevator."

Jerry and Kat both looked sheepish, and Slaäm chuckled quietly.

"Well, you're certainly not the first tourists to land without reading the manual. But most people don't try to sneak out the side gate, so we catch 'em before they can make fools of themselves. The outfitters in the ground station do quite a good business, I hear.

"Let me fill you in a bit on the history of our little planet. That might answer some of the questions you've probably got.

"You've noticed the total ban on technology of any kind, right? That's a consequence first of the planet itself, and then of the kind of people who were inspired to live here.

"Originally, when the first Retrievers landed here, they were stranded." Kat gave a little gasp, but Slaäm continued talking. "Three in a row, apparently. Found they couldn't reach orbit again and couldn't transmit any communications signals. They spent almost eight full years living off the land before a larger mining ship happened to pass by and came down to check out the geology."

"That was a bit of good luck. The bigger ship was able – just barely – to make it back out of the atmosphere and the planet was marked as a one-way destination.

"But at that time there were a few groups of people who were looking for exactly that quality in a planet. You know the types – Luddites, Anachronists, pioneer survivalists, etc. People who want to live in some timeframe or environment that they find romantic or appealing in some way, and don't want a constant stream of spacefaring visitors messing with their fantasy world.

"The ones who grabbed this planet were the hard-core 'Renaissance Faire' types who weren't content with spending the occasional weekend pretending they were living in medieval times, but wanted it 24/7/365.

"And when they settled the planet they nailed in place a very restrictive charter that forbids any modern technology, clothing or lifestyle that doesn't perfectly align with the period."

"I take it that doesn't include Space Elevators," said Jerry.

"Not so fast – that comes much later. About fifty years later, that is, when 90% of the population was starving and finding it almost impossible to grow edibles on this rock. Living life as a serf in the Dark Ages didn't seem so romantic anymore, and revolution was imminent.

"They were in trouble, and His Majesty King Godwin could see the writing on the wall. But he had an ace up his sleeve – this planet has two valuable things going for it: one is a rare mineral, and the other is an even rarer herb, found only on this world.

"The mineral you know as 'halladium' – about a century ago it replaced lithium as the preferred battery storage medium, and for good reason. It's the lightest and lease dense solid element ever discovered, and has electrochemical properties that are off the scale. Space travel probably wouldn't even be possible today without halladium batteries to power the Langstrom Drives. Problem is, mankind has already depleted almost all known sources of halladium, except for this world's strikingly high abundance.

"But that alone wasn't enough to entice the mining companies to come here. If you can't leave the planet, it doesn't matter how valuable your cargo is."

"Why can't ships leave the planet?" said Kat.

"Because of this system's star -- it generates an almost constant stream of coronal mass ejections, which result in a barrage of ion storms throughout the system. For this planet, even at 98 million miles distance, that's enough to produce intense upper-atmosphere geomagnetic storms, which in turn create vicious lower-atmospheric turbulence. Any ship attempting to pass through the atmosphere to reach orbit is torn apart by the physical turbulence. If by some miracle it survives that, it's fried by the geomagnetic assault that comes right after."

"Which would explain the Space Elevator," said Jerry.

"Exactly. In fact, the Elevator actually *benefits* from the intense geomagnetic forces – the cable acts as a gigantic lighting rod. It's coated with an extremely thin layer of hafnium diboride, which feeds the geomagnetic interference through the cable and acts to replace the heavy magnetic receptor coils normally found inside the rails of maglev trains and other similar systems. It's a perfect solution."

Slaäm paused to take a large swallow from his tankard of ale, and Kat and Jerry followed suit. The band was playing full force at the moment, but thankfully on the other side of the room. A small knot of dancing bodies in front of them absorbed enough of the sound to allow the little trio to maintain conversation at slightly less than shouting volumes.

"Is it always so raucous in here?" asked Kat.

"No, but you've come on Tourney Weekend – tens of thousands of people from all over the galaxy, along with a healthy portion of this planet's population, have come to see the jousting matches in the arena for the next three days. Until the tournament is over, this village is Party Central."

"We're going, right?" Kat asked Jerry. "Do you have tickets?"

"Yup. Two all-access passes are included with our room."

"That's good luck for you, Jer," said Slaäm. "These tourneys are sold-out for months in advance.

"In fact," he continued, "That's the other half of the equation that saved this planet's bacon.

"Remember I told you there were *two* very special properties to this planet? The second is a rare herb the scientists call *'Aggressonia piperium'*, but the rest of us just refer to as 'Aggresso'. All attempts to cultivate it off-world have failed. It doesn't travel well and doesn't produce seeds, and apparently needs some indefinable compound in this planet's biosphere in order to grow. Within 24 hours of being removed from its native environment it's as dead as King Tut."

"What makes it so special?" asked Jerry.

"It's a physical enhancement compound that is completely undetectable in the human body. You metabolize it immediately upon ingestion, and after that there's no test or scan that can find even the most miniscule amount in your bloodstream or tissues. It enhances your physical abilities by as much as 40%, depending how much you take, and how often."

"Why haven't I ever heard of this miracle drug before?"

"Because it's so undetectable. It's been banned universe-wide by the Association of Sporting Cooperatives.

"Sports is probably the most valuable commodity in all the known galaxies, Jerry. There's not a human alive who doesn't follow some kind of competitive activity, and a lot of those people bet on the events, as well. Put them together and you have an industry that generates revenues that dwarf any other product. Period.

"Now consider that any participant can take an herb that enhances their ability by as much as 40% -- without being detected. Poof! Disaster! No one would be interested in competitive sports anymore and betting would certainly dry up. You'd never know what your teams were going up against.

"When it became clear this planet would be enabling access to its treasures, the hammer came down from above, and a planetary quarantine on exports was imposed. Virtually every single molecule of matter leaving this planet's surface is scanned, examined and recorded. Trying to smuggle Aggresso off-world will land you thirty years in the slammer for your *first* attempt. They take this thing *very* seriously."

"That would explain the crazy inspection protocols up on the space station."

"Yup. There's no shipment or craft that arrives or departs that station without being probed right down to its nethers.

"But Aggresso is legal down here, planetside. And that's one reason the Tourney is so popular – it's an opportunity to see virtual supermen beating on each other in a series of deadly games. The Tourney broadcasts galaxy-wide on pay-per-view networks catering to people who like that sort of thing.

"When you put the two revenue streams together, you have just enough to cover the costs of running the Space Elevator, and in about fifty years' time it will have paid off the zero-interest construction loan the planet got from the Intergalactic Space Consortium to build the thing.

"There's just one problem, Jerry. I don't know how much you know about massive interstellar corporations, but in my experience, taking fifty years to essentially break even isn't a deal they tend to drool over.

"I think the Space Elevator people have found a way to… shall we say, *enhance* their operating revenues, and I'm a bit concerned. If you ask me, there's something rotten in the state of Denmark."

Jerry, Kat, and Slaäm sat quietly at their table, gazing down at their tankards, each lost in their own set of thoughts. For Slaäm, most of his concerns centered on the suspicions he harboured about his employer.

As for Jerry, he was wondering just how deeply he should draw his friend into the criminal conspiracy that had enmeshed him and Kat.

Kat worried mostly about Jerry, wondering if he'd absorbed any of what Slaäm had said or if he'd been too busy staring at her breasts to hear anything. She reflected that this outfit would be a good clothing choice the next time she needed to ask Jerry for a favour.

Finally, Jerry seemed to have made a decision.

"Slaäm, I'm glad you feel that way. There's actually something going on here that concerns me and Kat, and to be honest this isn't purely just a pleasure trip for us anymore. We might actually need your help."

"You don't say, Jerry," said Slaäm with a wry grin. "And here I thought it was just a coincidence that two violent deaths in the same day should occur just when you were passing through. Colour me surprised, my friend."

Jerry sat back in his chair and chuckled ruefully. "You always were a hard one to put anything by, Slaäm. But you need to take my word for it that Kat and I are unwilling participants in this mess, innocent bystanders who've gotten tangled up in something beyond our understanding."

"I believe you, Jerry. I know you're a straight shooter. And judging by the way you two have acted since you arrived, you obviously had no idea what you were stepping into. Tell me what you're involved in, though. I'll see if I can help you out somehow."

While Jerry filled in Slaäm on recent events, Kat reclined in her chair and discreetly scanned the room. Her Slimlines ran a facial recognition sweep on everyone present to check if any current attendees had been anywhere near them since the restaurant incident, but the scan came up blank. Kat breathed a bit easier, but nonetheless told her glasses to monitor and lip-read the faces in sight to check for incriminating conversations that might involve her and Jerry.

Jerry had finished bringing Slaäm up to speed, and paused for a moment to take a drink.

"That watch business sounds intriguing, Jer," said Slaäm. "Do you have it with you? I'd like to take a look at it."

"I do have it, it's in my pocket, but… I'm not sure I should openly display it in this room."

"Oh! Right you are, old friend – you got my curiosity going so hard I totally forgot what would happen if any of these neanderthals caught sight of it. Burning at the stake, I should imagine."

"Why don't we step outside for a moment," said Kat. "My head is throbbing from the noise and stale air in here. We can probably get a bit more privacy out on the rear terrace – I noticed earlier they have a beer garden out there. It's probably deserted at this time of night, especially in this weather."

"Good idea, hon. I'm getting hoarse talking over the music and the noise. I could use some air myself."

They got up from their table and made their way over to the patio doors at the back of the room, dodging barmaids and drunken patrons swirling around them. For the most part, no one paid them any attention, except for a group of delighted patrons who pounced on their abandoned table.

Kat's Slimlines spoke up, though: "There are three men at a table off to your right whose eyes are following us intently, Kat. But they haven't said anything."

Hopefully just a set of bored drunks checking out my rack.

Her glasses displayed an image of the men and she caught her breath to note that all three were dressed in identical long brown leather trench coats.

After enduring the close atmosphere in the pub room, the fresh chill of the night air was an invigourating delight. They found a little wooden table tucked beneath a slatted bower at the rear of the garden and they stood in a tight knot beside it.

"Say, Slaäm," said Kat quietly, "what do you know about the men who dress in long brown trench coats? I've seen several of them since arriving. Are they part of a cult or something?"

"Well, you could almost say that, Kat. They're members of the hard-core segment of this population.

"As you might expect, in the last several decades since this planet was settled, a dozen new generations of people have been born here and not everyone is delighted to find themselves stuck in a stone-age society. They don't quite know exactly what they're missing, since they have zero contact with the rest of the galaxy, including a complete blackout on off-world communications of any kind. They don't even know what the ground station looks like on the inside – it's been designed to resemble a huge castle from the outside, and planetary residents aren't allowed inside the gates.

"But they know there's a lot more galaxy out there and many of the people born into this environment barely tolerate the lifestyle that's been forced on them.

"But then you have your True Believers, and they're the ones who keep this planet mired in millennia-old traditions and lifestyle, and that's where your trench-coat-clan comes in. They refuse to speak modern English and reject even the slightest attempts to introduce creature comforts. They won't even allow proper water purification facilities to be built, and as a consequence thousands of people die each year from cholera and other water-borne diseases. And forget about doctors, of course. If you get sick here, you usually die."

Kat and Jerry were understandably horrified.

"That's awful!" said Kat. "That's so barbaric! How…."

"'Medieval'?" said Slaäm. "Exactly."

"Can't the planet's rulers allow some modernizations to creep in?" asked Jerry.

"The planet's rulers are where the problems begin, Jer. They're firmly on the side of the Anachronists, even though they themselves live lives of sumptuous luxury. A lot of them have off-world homes and spend the majority of their time there, but keep an iron grip on their power here while sucking up profits from the mining and sporting revenues.

"And if what I suspect is going on turns out to be true, there's even more dirty money flowing into hidden offworld bank accounts. The rot runs deep here, I think.

"Which reminds me, let's take a look at that watch, Jerry. Let's see what's so special about it."

Jerry pulled the watch out from a pocket on his leather jerkin and was about to hand it to Slaäm when he said, "Oops, hold on – that's the wrong watch. This is *my* watch – it's a Patek Philippe. The watch we want is this one," and he pulled out from a different pocket another slim gold timepiece.

"This is an Audemars-Piguet. They're quite similar, actually, both are a few hundred years old, and in the twentieth century they ran around several hundred thousand dollars apiece. Very rare now, I imagine. I can't begin to guess what a collector would offer for either one."

"How much is a hundred thousand dollars in today's credits, Jer?" asked Kat. When he told her she caught her breath and started coughing viciously. As he patted her on the back she looked up at him and said, "And you have the nerve to complain about how much I spent on my Slimlines!"

"Hey, I didn't *buy* my watch – I won it in a wager with my grandfather. I think he was pretty pissed off to give it up, but he handed it over nonetheless. Surprised me, too. He was an especially miserly old bird. I think this was the first thing of value he ever willingly parted with, at least as long as I knew him."

Jerry handed his watch to Kat to look at while Slaäm examined the dead man's timepiece.

"I dunno, Jerry. It's hard to tell in this dim light, but it doesn't look like the watch case itself has been opened – you can see a little bit of corrosion on the lugs, and that would have been worn off if they'd been unscrewed. And the crystal looks flawless. But again, this isn't the best light for an inspection. Would you be okay with me taking it back to my office and examining it with some modern equipment?"

"Be my guest, Slaäm – it's not doing me any good sitting in my pocket."

Slaäm discreetly slipped the timepiece into a vest pocket in his jacket and turned to say something to Kat when he noticed she was standing frozen in place.

"Um, Kat? Are you okay? Jerry? What's going on?"

Kat put her fingers to her lips and kept standing stock still.

"Don't move, you two," she whispered. "My Slimlines have detected someone dressed in black up on the roof over to our left. We're being watched.

"Here, Jerry," she hissed, "take your watch back and try to act natural. I'm going to see if my glasses can make out any details."

Jerry and Slaäm did their best to casually step back and pretend to talk about something meaningless, while Kat innocently gazed up at the stars above, all the while monitoring the enhanced images of their watchers displayed in her lenses.

Suddenly, she threw herself forward and tackled Jerry, knocking him off-balance and over the table. In the next split second a hard thud came from the direction of the wall to their right, followed immediately by a softer, squishier sound behind her. She looked up from where she lay sprawled across the table to see a long, thin arrow protruding from Slaäm's body, and watched in horror as he crumpled to the ground beside her.

10

RANTICALLY, JERRY CRAWLED on all fours beneath the table and grasped Slaäm's shoulders, pulling him out of sight of their attackers.

"Slaäm! Can you hear me? Slaäm!" he hissed, trying to get a good look at the man. The arrow protruded several inches from his body, but Jerry couldn't tell precisely where it had impacted.

"Ohhhh, Good Lord, Jerry, that hurts!" groaned Slaäm. "It feels like a line of fire is burning in me."

"Where did it get you? Did it puncture any major organs?"

"No, no…. It's not too bad, all things considered…. It got my arm. I think my biceps has been impaled."

Jerry took a closer look and saw that Slaäm was right. The arrow was buried in his left arm, half of it sticking out the back side, and the other half protruding out the front.

"Thank God for that!" said Kat. "But we need to get you to a doctor. That's a vicious wound."

"No doctors here, remember?" said Slaäm with a weak smile. "If I can make it back to the station we have a full hospital on site. But first I have to make it there. The next arrow might make this wound look minor."

"I don't think any more arrows are on their way," said Kat. "Whoever the shooter – or shooters – are, they vamoosed as soon as we hit the dirt. If we can make it out to the street, we should be able to find a carriage you can take back to the station. I just don't know about walking through that beer hall with that bolt sticking out of your wing. There might be questions and I don't want to get you involved."

"I think this defines pretty serious involvement already, Kat," said Jerry, eyeing the length of wood protruding from Slaäm's arm.

"You know what I mean. If Slaäm can get back to the station in one piece he might be able to pass this off as an unfortunate accident caused by pre-tourney hijinx. I don't think he was the intended target, anyways."

"You're probably right about that," said Jerry, looking over at the shaft buried in the wall beside him. "If you hadn't tackled me when you did, that wall would still be in excellent condition."

"C'mon, let's get Slaäm to his feet. I notice there's a thin passageway alongside the building. I think we can get to the street that way."

Quickly, the group filed into the narrow gap alongside the hotel, and Kat and Slaäm stayed tucked in the shadows while Jerry flagged down a covered carriage. When it was opposite them, Slaäm discreetly slipped out of the shadows and into the wagon. Jerry latched the door behind him and walked up to the driver's perch.

He gave the driver a five-credit note, which had the man uttering exclamations of astonishment, but Jerry cut him off and told him to get to the ground station as fast as his carriage would allow. No sooner had he stopped speaking than the carriage burst into movement, and within seconds disappeared out of sight down the cobblestone-covered street.

Jerry turned back to the hotel entrance and pulled open the door for Kat, who slipped inside and quickly scanned the crowd still filling the pub. The three trench-coat-clad men who had been sitting there earlier were now absent, and no one else so much as glanced in their direction.

The Innkeeper raised his eyebrows a bit when he saw Jerry and Kat come in. "Good even, my friends," he said. "I hadn't realised you had left the premises. I didn't see you go out. Is there something you were looking for? We try to maintain a full-service establishment here. I assure you that whatever you seek, we can surely provide."

"No, we're fine, thank you," said Jerry. "We just needed a breath of fresh air. But now that you mention it, a bit of food might be nice. We haven't had the chance to eat yet. Can you have a couple of trays sent up to our suite?"

"Of course! Did you have anything specific in mind?"

"Um, maybe some Shepherd's Pie and Bangers and Mash? Along with a couple tankards of ale?"

"Excellent choice, Milord. I shall have two trays sent up forthwith."

"I can't wait to shed this dress, Jer," said Kat as they made their way up the stairs, but seeing the evil grin on his face she quickly added, "and not for that reason, you one-track monster. The corset is cinched so tight I feel like my insides are being squeezed like fresh sausage. I'm telling you, even on his best days Torquemada had nothing on the designers of these garments."

When they opened the door to their suite they both stood dumbfounded, frozen to the spot. Their luggage, their new clothes, the bedding and all the furniture in the room had been tossed and emptied and left in complete disarray.

"Those bastards," said Kat softly. "And to think I wasted my time making the bed before we left."

"I *told* you not to bother with that," said Jerry, tentatively stepping into the room and turning upright a small side table that lay in his way.

"Judging from the mess they left, it doesn't look like they found what they were looking for, Jer."

"Probably because it was in my pocket, Kat. Here – give me a hand with the bed. We'll need somewhere to put the trays of food when they arrive."

"Just like that? You're just going to settle down in our ruined bedroom and eat like nothing happened?"

"No, first I'm going to drain the tankard of ale that will be here momentarily, *then* I'm going to eat. I've had a hard night, Kat. A messy room is the least of my concerns."

"JERRY, HOW ARE WE going to get any kind of sleep tonight if we're sitting ducks in this medieval shooting gallery?" asked Kat through a mouthful of bangers and mash.

"Well, in my day the trick would be to lay crumpled newspapers all over the floor by the room's windows and door, but I imagine you have slightly more elegant methods, right, Kat?"

"Um, well, I suppose I could leave my Slimlines on the night-table beside the bed, and if they detect any noise or intrusions, they'll sound an alarm in my head that should provide plenty of warning."

"Perfect! I'll close the shutters to prevent any projectiles entering through the window, and we can sleep like babies without a care in the world."

Kat eyed him sideways and said, "You're taking this pretty casually for someone who almost became a human pincushion."

"That silly incident? Oh, piffle, Kat. That sort of thing doesn't upset me in the least. You know, I try not to let the little things in life bother me. You should try it sometimes – you're always so tense these days." And he chuckled contentedly.

Kat just rolled her eyes skyward and ate another forkful of her meal. *Men can be* so *tedious*, she thought.

11

**HE NIGHT PASSED UNEVENTFULLY,**
and come morning Jerry slipped
downstairs early to change some credit
notes into local coin of the realm, and then
ordered two breakfast trays to be sent up.

"Wake up, Kat – there's food here."

Rubbing her eyes, Kat groggily scanned the room, and
finally turned to Jerry and said, "Tell me it's just an optical
illusion that the sun hasn't come up yet."

"Heh heh, it's no illusion. But Tourney starts about two
hours after dawn, and I figure you'll need at least one of those
hours just to get dressed. Up and at 'em, sleepyhead," and
giving her a forceful push, he rolled her off the bed and onto
the floor.

"Yow! Jerry! What the heck is wrong with you?"

Laughing heartily, he said between guffaws, "How quickly
they forget! Not so funny when someone is pushing *you* off
the bed, is it?"

"You could have just *asked* me to get up! You didn't have
to roll me onto the floor."

"Hey, sweetie – what's good for the goose is good for the
goose's girlfriend."

"That's not how that expression works, Jerry."

"It is when the goose is the one laughing."

Fortunately for Kat, she had left both her heavy boots on the floor beside the bed, so she had something to throw at Jerry as he howled and ducked away.

It wasn't hard to find the arena. It seemed that every person in the village was headed in the same direction, noisily chattering and laughing as they made their way through the streets and up a small hill to a large field gaily festooned with colourful pennants. Food and souvenir vendors were everywhere, and little groups of children ran back and forth, batting at each other with small wooden swords or wrestling in the dirt.

Thankfully, the weather had noticeably improved and there wasn't a cloud in sight. Even though it was still early morning, the sun was already blazing quite intensely in the sky. Kat started to worry that she would be emerging from their day's activities with a complexion more suited to a lobster.

At the far end of the field a large outdoor amphitheater was surrounded with lines of people slowly making their way inside through various wide arched gates.

When Jerry and Kat arrived at a gate, a guard took one look at their passes and said, "Prithee, Milord, come hither, thy place is nae with this crowd of ruffians."

Leading them through the maelstrom of pushing and shoving bodies inside the entrance gate, he brutally plowed a path to a staircase that ascended to the second level of the seats, and over to a small group of luxury boxes shielded from the sun by large canvas coverings supported by long poles. Jerry pressed a small copper-coloured coin into the man's hand. The guard bowed gratefully and hustled back to his post.

"Ooh, Jerry, this looks awesome," said Kat, happily scanning the enormous arena while she settled into her chair. "You didn't tell me we were sitting with the royalty."

Jerry glanced around at the other patrons, most of whom were wearing gilded purple and red tunics and silk hose.

"I think I'm a little underdressed, though, Kat. Maybe I shouldn't have chosen this leather jerkin and breeches."

"You're just feeling self-conscious, Jer. Once you get settled you'll forget all about it, especially when you've had a chance to leer at all the women's chests."

A fat, balding man of about sixty years and a buxom damsel in her twenties entered the loge and took their seats next to Kat. The man pointedly leered at Kat's barely-concealed breasts shining up at him from over her skimpy festival dress.

"Ah… hail… good, ah, good lord. Fair tidings, I bid thee," said Kat tentatively.

"Screw that gobbledygook, honey – my babe and I are just here for the show."

"Oh, what a relief," said Kat. "I'm not sure I could keep that up for very long."

"That stuff is all just bullshit, if you ask me. It's nice to meet you – my name's Melvin. Melvin Zimmerman. Maybe you've heard of me before – the Gefilte Fish King of Bethel Andromedae? This is Betsy, my main squeeze" – here the young lass giggled pleasantly – "We come here every year to watch the mayhem. One of the last places in the galaxy where you can still watch people actually beat each other to death. None of that pussy 'stop the fight' crap here – no quarter asked, no quarter given. They carry the losers out feet first."

Kat visibly paled. "You can't be serious. They actually *kill* each other?"

"Well sure – that's the whole appeal. They're all hopped-up on that drug of theirs and they just go at it pedal-to-the-metal. No-holds-barred action, and only one left standing."

Kat looked a little green and turned to Jerry and said, "I'm not sure I want to stick around for this, Jer."

"Just let's give it a look, Kat. It might not be all blood and guts. English jousting wasn't designed to actually *kill* the combatants. The most they usually did was de-horse their opponent."

"Haw, not in this place, buddy," said Melvin from over Kat's shoulder. "This place has more in common with the Roman Coliseum than any namby-pamby British royal games, I can tell you that!"

"It's really lots of fun," added Betsy, leaning over Melvin and bending over slightly, the better to display a pair of unusually large breasts, which looked even more impressive by virtue of her low-cut gown. The bodice lifted her ample cleavage high enough to display the top half of her nipples, both of which were painted with bright red lipstick.

She paused a moment to do her own bit of leering at Kat's bosom, even more overtly than her partner had.

"And after the games Melvin and I like to invite a few special friends over to our hotel suite for some… after-tourney fun… if you know what I mean…."

Kat hoped with all her heart that she *didn't* actually know what the woman meant, and she slowly turned away and murmured to Jerry under her breath, "When you get up to go to the bathroom you and I are swapping seats."

Jerry just chuckled. "As long as that's all we'll be swapping today, Kat."

She punched him in the arm. Hard.

THE FIRST HOUR or so wasn't too bad, as far as Kat was concerned. There was a lot of blowing of trumpets and "Hail thee"s and "Hail thou"s and the like, and then the King and Queen came in and took their seats. Meanwhile, some jugglers and acrobats and a halfway-decent magician put on a couple of shows to warm people up.

But then it started to get weird.

Two wagons were wheeled into the arena, each carrying a large cage holding a scantily-clad young female.

"Help me! Please the Lord, help!" screamed the women.

Immediately the crowd started roaring and many in the stands began calling out enthusiastically. Kat looked at Jerry quizzically, and he just shrugged.

Against her better judgment, Kat leaned to her left and said to Melvin, raising her voice to be heard over the cheering crowd, "What's going on here?"

"It's how each day of the tourney begins," he answered. "They're supposed to be witches who've been sentenced to death. In a minute the women will be pushed out of their cages and then a couple of vicious beasts will be herded into the arena. Then things start to really heat up."

"This can't really be happening," replied Kat.

"Oh, don't worry, honey, it's not what you think – just sit back and watch the show. You'll be surprised."

Once the wagons were in place at one end of the arena, two huge men came up to the cages and unlatched the doors, then dragged the women out by their hair, and threw them onto the dirt behind the wagons, which then were driven back out of the arena through one of several gates in the perimeter wall. The cheers got even louder.

Almost immediately, two enormous creatures rumbled into the arena. They looked like a cross between a rhinoceros and a wild boar, except their hides consisted of heavy plates of natural armour deep red in colour that extended along their back and sides. Two gigantic tusks adorned the sides of their heads, with a third vicious-looking spike protruding from their foreheads.

Upon entering the arena, both beasts threw their heads back and started roaring in terrifying bass tones, clearly audible even over the thunderous cheering of the crowd, and flung their heads back and forth.

Both the beasts looked in pain, and as they cast their heads from side to side they stumbled in ragged lines into the arena.

"What's wrong with those animals?" said Kat. "Something about them doesn't look natural."

"It's those harnesses they've got strapped around their necks and across their haunches," replied Melvin. "They're too dangerous to allow into the arena without being hobbled. Those harnesses have sharp spikes on their undersides, and when the creatures try to walk the spikes dig into them."

"Oh my God," said Kat, horrified. "That's so cruel! Is that really necessary?"

"You better believe it honey, unless you want to be trampled and gored where you sit. If they weren't wearing those harnesses, they could leap over the arena walls right into the stands and crush and devour us all."

The two women were still screaming, calling out to God and the Saints for mercy, and the beasts in the arena started to move closer to them.

"See how the monsters keep flinging their heads from side to side?" said Melvin. "They're tracking the women purely by sound and smell. That's because they're nocturnal and are almost blind in the bright sun. The light enrages them and sends them into a killing frenzy. We're going to have some real fun now, I tell ya."

Kat wanted to get up and leave right at that moment but Jerry's firm grip on her hand made her sit still while the tableau unfolded.

The women were shrieking for help, the beasts were howling and snorting as they pawed their way closer to the two terrified females, and the crowd was screaming at an almost fever pitch.

Suddenly, just as the beasts had drawn to within a meter of the women, two muscular men carrying long pikes and short axes and dressed in loincloths burst into the arena from one of the gates, and thundered over to the women. A deafening roar went up from the crowd, with many people looking like they were on the verge of hysteria.

The men leaped to the women's sides and threw them each an axe. No longer cowering or screaming for help, the women caught the weapons and raised them triumphantly above their heads.

The crowd roared even louder, which Kat had not thought possible, and then started calling out bloodthirsty oaths as the four humans leapt up and attacked the gigantic beasts.

A tremendous cheer shook the arena as one of the women leapt onto the back of one of the creatures and brought her axe down onto its head. She repeated the motion over and over while it staggered from side to side and howled in pain and anger. Finally, she split the skull, spilling brains and blood onto herself and the ground beneath her feet. The beast collapsed and lay still.

The other beast was spinning in a frenzy as the two men and the other woman alternately gored it with their pikes or slashed at its muzzle with the axe.

The first woman rejoined the group and the four humans pummeled it with a merciless barrage of blows. One of the men took his pike and, hefting it over his head, drove it straight through the animal's mouth and pierced its palate, the tip emerging from the top of its skull. The creature uttered an ear-shattering roar of pain and then collapsed, dead, at their feet.

The crowd was beyond itself with excitement. The people in the stands screeched and howled and cheered. Kat saw one young man who had been driven to such intense paroxysms of bloodlust he was rending his own garments and literally foaming at the mouth.

As the crowd began to quiet and the carcasses of the dead beasts were dragged out of the arena by a team of horses, Melvin leaned over to Kat and said, "That was just a warm-up. Now the *real* tourney begins."

"Maybe for you, dickwad, but not for us," she said grimly, standing up.

"Come on Jerry. We're leaving this hell-hole. *Now.*"

AT WAS SHAKING with outrage as she stormed out of the arena and across the pageant field.

"Oh. My. Ghod. Jerry, that was so awful I don't have words to express my feelings! What kind of barbaric, savage, cruel monsters are these people who live here?

"I was starting to feel sorry for them," she continued, gathering speed. "What with their feudal living conditions and foul environment, but this – *this* is beyond forgiveness! These people all deserve to be drawn and quartered and fed to the wild animals. What a pathetic collection of savages! And they have the *nerve* to call themselves Christians!"

"Now now, Kat, 'don't judge, lest ye be judged', right?... After all—"

"Don't *even*, Jerry. There's nothing you can say that could excuse that act of pure unmitigated animal torture we just witnessed. And did you see how they reacted? I think a lot of them were disappointed the animals died so soon."

A huge roar thundered out just then from the arena, and Kat's lip curled in disgust.

"All I can say is I hope that was one of the humans getting some of his own medicine. At first I was horrified to consider that they actually kill each other there, but now as far as I'm concerned, the fewer of them left alive at the end of this weekend, the better."

"I'm sensing a feeling of disapproval, Kat. I could be misreading you, though…."

Seeing the wry grin on Jerry's face, Kat visibly softened, relaxing her shoulders and producing a little rueful smile of her own.

"OK, Jer, I get the point. I need to let it go."

She drew closer to him and tucked her head against his shoulder.

"What would I do without you to bring me back to Earth, Jer?"

"Hey, I love your passion. I just think you need to keep in mind that old line about having the serenity to accept the things you can't change. These games have been going on for decades and we're powerless to stop them."

"That doesn't mean we can't make a difference, Jerry."

"Maybe yes, maybe no, Kat, but I think right now we've got a slightly more urgent matter we should be focusing on."

Kat's eyes suddenly snapped into focus.

"The watch! We should see how Slaäm is making out deciphering it."

"Exactly. Why don't we swing on over to the ground station and drop in on our buddy? I'll buy you an ice cream while we're there and this whole ugly morning will be just a bad memory for you, hon."

"Inshallah, Jer."

"Amen to that, Kat."

JERRY AND KAT felt self-conscious entering the ground station dressed in 14th century clothing, but relaxed when they saw they were far from alone in that regard. Most of the restaurants and shops were done up in pseudo-Middle Ages decor, with fake Old English menus or placards in front of their shops. One or two even made their staff dress in medieval garb, which some of the employees did *not* look happy about.

"This reminds me of the shops and restaurants in Disneyland, Jerry, like the Pirates of the Caribbean restaurant or the old-timey shops on Main Street."

"Yeah, I guess it's to help the tourists feel like they're getting the actual experience without any of the downside, like mud and warm beer."

"Why do I feel, though, that everyone is staring at me?"

"Well, I suspect it's partially due to your bodice," said Jerry, grinning wickedly. "But probably also because there's almost no other tourists here right now. Look how deserted this place is. Everyone is at the Tourney, except for people here doing business, and the station personnel, who probably wish they didn't have to be here right now, either. Let's get a quick snack then go hunt down Slaäm.

"Ooh, look, Kat! Roast turkey legs! Just like at the food booths at the Tourney, except minus the e. coli and the parasites! Let's go get a couple. Ooh! And cold beer!"

Kat just rolled her eyes and smiled. This really *was* starting to feel more and more like a trip to Disneyland….

THEY FOUND SLAÄM in his office looking just as he had the day before, with the obvious difference being that his left arm was now in a sling.

"I love the doctors here, Jerry," he said ebulliently. "They did such a good job it's as though I was never injured at all. The sling is mostly for show, as far as I'm concerned."

"Oh, I'm so happy to hear that, Slaäm. I feel so bad about getting you involved in all of this."

"You didn't, Jerry. I could have walked away when you told me your story, but this stuff is taking place in *my* house. If there are rats onboard, it's a lot more my problem than it is yours. I should be apologizing to you and not the other way around."

"Well, let's stop apologizing to each other and get down to brass tacks. Have you had a chance to examine the watch yet?"

"I have, and you're going to like what you hear. But hold on a moment –" Walking over to the glass wall of his office, he pushed a button and the wall became opaque.

"Prying eyes, you know. Can't be too careful, especially considering what's involved here."

"What *is* involved, Slaäm?" asked Kat impatiently. "I can't bear the suspense."

"Bottom line, Kat? It's money. Lots of it.

"The data you gave me details an extensive smuggling operation that's been operating under everyone's noses on this station for several years now, and the trail goes to the very top."

"Are you sure the data's good?" asked Jerry. "This could be an elaborate hoax, created to embarrass people, nothing more."

"I doubt it, Jerry. The technology used to encode the data on that watch is real high-tech stuff, nothing to sneeze at.

"At first, I couldn't detect anything unusual about the watch at all. And I'm betting you scanned it with those special glasses of yours, too, right Kat?"

"Yeah, but a full-spectrum scan still didn't turn up anything useful."

"That's because this is very unusual technology. I was wrong last night about the watch case not having been opened. Someone opened it verrrry carefully, and pretty recently, as far as I can tell, but that's a blind alley anyways. I found the data purely by accident when I got desperate and scanned the whole unit with an electron microscope. The data's not *in* the watch, Jerry – it's burned into the actual watch crystal."

"But that's not so unusual, Slaäm. We've been storing data in crystal for centuries."

"Not like this, Jerry. I've only read about this technology. I didn't think it was possible. It created a 9-dimensional storage array that's written with a zeptosecond laser."

"Zeptosecond? I don't know that one."

"A zeptosecond is a trillionth of a billionth of a second. A zeptosecond laser fires in zeptosecond pulses to create a storage matrix in the crystal, which is actually nanostructured glass. And it is, for all intents and purposes, eternal. The crystal in that watch will actually outlast the projected age of the universe."

"Ow. I'm getting a headache," said Kat.

"You and me both," said Slaäm. "This technology was originally formulated all the way back in the early 2000's, but back then it was about as attainable as unravelling the layers of matter described in string theory."

"But why couldn't my glasses detect the data written onto the crystal? They should have picked up the holoimaging immediately."

"Except this isn't holoimaging, Kat. This data can only be read with a combination of a molecular-level microscope and a polarizer. Which, fortunately, I have in my lab."

"What did you do with the data? I hope you made a copy."

"Jerry, do I look like I'm an idiot? *Of course* I made a copy. In fact," he said, tapping a button on a console on his desk, "if you want to, Kat, you can sync with my system and download your own copy right now."

"Already done, Slaäm. My Slimlines grabbed it the second you opened the link."

He chuckled and said, "Those things are nothing less than amazing, Kat. If you ever want to get rid of them…."

Kat just laughed and winked at him.

"Sure thing, Slaäm. You'll be the first one I call. After they pry them out of my cold, dead fingers, of course."

"Oh, Jerry – before I forget, let me give you back that watch. I really don't want to keep it here on the premises."

"I can't say I blame you for that, Slaäm. It was courageous bringing it here to begin with."

Slaäm went over to a wall safe discreetly tucked behind a decorative panel in his office wall and tapped a code, then extracted the watch, which he turned to hand to Jerry. At that exact moment, his office door swung open and a man poked his head in.

"Boss, if you have a mo—" and then stopped as he saw the watch in Jerry's hand.

"Wow, that's a nice looking watch," he said.

"Um, yeah, family heirloom," said Jerry as he dropped it into a pocket on his leather jerkin.

"Well, Chief, I just wanted to tell you we're all waiting on you so we can run this month's cable stress test. So whenever you have a minute…."

"Right, I'll be out in a sec, Wilkins. Close the door behind you, okay?"

"Oh, right, sorry Chief. Right – I mean, thank you, Chief," and the flustered engineer quickly pulled the door shut and disappeared.

"Is that going to be a problem?" said Jerry, frowning.

"Wilkins? Oh, no, he's a stand-up guy. Only been here about six months and he's already become my right-hand man. Came to us from the Fusion Research Center on Tesla Prime. There's little chance he's involved in this mess.

"Say, Jerry, Kat – I have to go do this thing, but there's still a lot more I want to go over with you guys. Let's have lunch before you leave the station. Meet me here in an hour," he said, scribbling a name on a small piece of paper and handing it to Kat.

As Kat and Jerry left Slaäm's office Kat raised her voice and said loudly to Jerry, reading from the paper he had given her, "Slaäm has awful handwriting Jerry, but I think this says 'Mama Sofia's'. Apparently that's at almost the opposite end of the station. I wish he'd chosen something closer."

"Well, maybe we can take in some of the sights along the way and do some shopping enroute, Kat."

"Great idea, Jer. After all, we do have to kill two full hours till our meeting."

As they trotted away down the corridors beneath the station, Jerry said, "That was a nice bit of play-acting, Kat. Wanna tell me what was going on back there? Don't tell me you're worried about Wilkins."

"No, I trust Slaäm's judgment, Jerry. I'm more concerned about the technician who was working at the Hydrostatic Sensor Array opposite Slaäm's office – the fellow had a clear line of sight into the office when the door opened."

"Yeah, so? Why would that set off alarm bells?"

"Two reasons, Jerry. One, my Slimlines immediately tagged him as sitting three tables away from us in the pub room last night when we were drinking with Slaäm. And two, the monitoring station he was supposedly working at was in standby mode. With any luck, he won't bother trying to follow us so we don't accidentally spot him, but instead he'll just show up at Mama Sofia's in two hours – I had my glasses find me a restaurant far away from where we're actually going. And I hope he's hungry, because there won't be much else for him to do there but order lunch."

"Wow, Kat. I'm really impressed."

"Well c'mon, Jer. I *told* you I'm not just another pretty face. Now, weren't you saying something earlier about going shopping...?"

THE TECHNICIAN LEFT his workstation and wandered away once Kat and Jerry had passed out of sight. Slipping into a utility closet situated in a side corridor, he tapped an earbud and made contact with his associates.

"He's got the watch, alright," reported the man. "It's the same one I saw the girl hand him last night on the patio. I saw him slip it into his pocket not five minutes ago. I think he was showing it to the Head of Engineering. They probably can't read the data, if they can find it at all. Whatever the problem is, though, it doesn't look like his Engineering friend can help him with it, so he held on to it."

The man paused a moment and listened to his confederates.

"No, they left right afterwards," he replied. "But I know where they're going. They're going to meet with their other contacts in two hours at Mama Sofia's in the north quadrant. Get Xi Tung and Luis and meet me across from the restaurant in an hour and forty-five. And bring *guns* this time. With scopes. Fuck that ridiculous bow-and-arrow shit. This time no one walks away, and screw the consequences. We're jamming the lid down on this affair once and for all."

THE SPOT SLAÄM had chosen for their lunch rendezvous was tucked-away at the end of an alley that bled off the main concourse. Not only was it almost deserted, the establishment offered little private enclosed booths for diners seeking an extra helping of anonymity.

"I'm surprised the owner of this place can keep it going," Jerry said to Slaäm when they were all together in one of the booths and eating lunch. "I think we're the only patrons here."

"Well, right now most people are at the Tourney, Jerry, but even during normal times this place depends mostly on 'special' customers. If you're looking for privacy for any reason – legal or otherwise – this is the place to come."

Slaäm nodded at a little green light embedded in the table.

"That's a bug detector and jammer all in one. Electronic eavesdropping can't happen here. If you're here to hash out a top-secret business deal, or to meet your paramour or hooker, or simply to evade unwelcome publicity if you happen to be a celebrity or a politician, you can be confident that what happens in the booth stays in the booth."

"We used to have an entire city on Earth that made that claim."

"But back then it was more of an aspiration than a guarantee, I believe. Here, it's this place's bread-and-butter. Maybe the owner could be bribed if the number were big enough, but no one knew we were coming here so I doubt that's an issue right now.

"And no one followed me, either. I took the service corridors underground and came in through the kitchen. And knowing you two as I do, I'll bet you did the same thing."

Jerry chuckled and nodded. "And Kat's Slimlines have blocked us from the station's surveillance systems, so I think we're good here."

"Let's get down to it, then."

"I TOLD YOU that this involves smuggling," said Slaäm, between sips from a large tankard of ale, "But you'll be surprised by how far it goes and the numbers involved.

"The data file on the watch is insanely comprehensive and detailed. Every transaction, vessel, smuggler, government official, bribe, purchaser, purchase amount and everything else down to the last microgram of product is listed, with dates going back almost fifteen years. This operation runs *deep*, like the corruption, and the records clearly implicate the planet's rulers along with senior Elevator management. The only parties that seem not to be involved are the Space Station personnel and management."

"Wait," said Kat. "Aren't the Elevator and Space Station one and the same? You mean they're two different companies?"

"That's right, Kat. It was set up that way partly to prevent this exact problem from occurring. The station was seen as the last line of defense. That's why the Elevator and ground station don't have security worth shit and don't bother passengers with anything more than the most cursory scan. It's the station that controls what passes in or out of this system. It's the bottleneck that everyone – and everything – has to pass through.

"It's owned and operated by the Sports Consortium, and they change up most of the senior management every six months or so, often enough to prevent corruption from setting in. It's a good plan and it works as intended, apparently. And aside from one cryptic entry, none of the data I found implicates or involves them in the least."

"What do you mean, 'cryptic'?" asked Jerry.

"The only participant where the data lists just a code ID instead of a name. It's 'SS1'. That sounds an awful lot to me like shorthand for 'Space Station 1', but who it refers to is never revealed. It's possible it's a rotating ID that designates whoever they have in the station working for them at various times. The station rotates personnel pretty frequently and they might need to buy off the replacements whenever someone new takes over the position."

Jerry looked at Slaäm dubiously.

"I still can't imagine what could be smuggled off this planet that would merit the lucrative financial rewards you've alluded to, Slaäm. I can't believe a few dozen crooked athletes buying a banned substance could generate more than a few thousand credits, at most. And there's nothing else on this planet that's worth more than dirt, aside from the halladium they're already mining."

"Take my word for it, Jerry, they're smuggling Aggresso, alright. But it's not athletes who are willing to pay millions of credits for it.

"I know I told you that sports is the galaxy's most lucrative business, but what other well-established enterprise offers obscene profits for ruthless individuals?"

Kat and Jerry glanced at each other, then shrugged. They came up blank.

"It's *war*, guys. Good, old-fashioned, shoot-'em-up, burn the cities and kill the population War.

"War?" asked Kat in astonishment. "But there's no war anymore! Once nuclear and chemical weapons were banned along with autonomous military robotics, and we started finding more habitable planets than we know what to do with, war pretty-well went the way of the Dodo."

Jerry smiled to hear Kat use one of his favourite expressions.

"Well, yes and no, Kat," said Slaäm. "Certainly, inter-planetary war is off the table, and when it comes to conflict with other parties on your own planet, duking it out with your neighbours mano-a-mano on the battlefield is a dubious proposition, but that's only because no one has a clear advantage when you're fighting fair.

"But if you could somehow juice up your troops into super soldiers just long enough to stomp your enemies to pulp, that opens the door to potentially trillions of credits in booty – seized factories, banking reserves, natural resources that don't require importation from some faraway planet, you get the gist of it.

"Earlier today I looked up the last twenty major single-planet armed conflicts fought in the galaxy. Most were on smaller, obscure worlds that no one pays much attention to, but I'll tell you the one thing they all had in common: the victorious countries in every one of those wars was on the list of purchasers in our data file."

"Which means…" said Jerry, "The people who are moving this stuff offworld are actively marketing it to despots and warlords – and probably fomenting war just to drive sales."

"Exactly," replied Slaäm. "In precisely the same way international arms merchants used to stoke regional conflicts back on Earth in the twentieth and twenty-first centuries."

Kat sat back heavily in her chair with a look of disgust. "I wish I could say this shocks me, but after what I witnessed in the arena this morning, it fits perfectly. The people on this planet are nothing more than cruel, vicious, bloodthirsty animals. Manipulating whole populations into committing mass murder just to make a few bucks seems right up their alley."

"It's not the people who are doing this, babe – it's the corrupt upper class and their politicians."

"The apple doesn't fall far from the tree, Jerry. This entire planet is a plague on the galaxy and needs to be wiped off the map, as far as I'm concerned."

"Well, Slaäm," said Jerry, "That's the who and the what of it. Now tell us how. If the space station isn't complicit in this, how are the smugglers getting the Aggresso into interplanetary transit?"

"That's where the clues run out, Jerry. For all the detailed transactional data in these records, there's not one word about how they're doing it. I was hoping maybe you had some ideas.

Maybe you and I could put our heads together and puzzle this thing out."

Jerry looked at him blankly, and then both men jumped at the snort that burst forth from Kat.

"Well, fellas, looks like we've got ourselves a real mystery here," said Kat. "And I think I know just how to go about solving it."

Both men looked at her in astonishment.

"Aww, wassamatta, boys? Weren't expecting the girls to want to play, too?

JERRY AND KAT sat in the carriage as it bounced its way to the Coughing Cat, and the silence hung heavy between them.

It was obvious Jerry was still mad at her, and he sulkily stared out the little window as they teetered along.

"Pouting really isn't helpful, Jer."

"Isn't it, Kat? Is it less helpful than, oh, I don't know – keeping it to myself when I spot the one person who got us into all this mess?"

"I didn't 'keep it to myself', Jer. I just waited for an appropriate time to share. We've had our hands pretty full today, you know. I saw no point in rushing off half-cocked."

"It's not half-cocked when both our lives are hanging in the balance, Kat."

"Potato patahto, Jerry. I let you know when it was germane. It's not as though we could have confronted her in the middle of the tournament and given her the third degree. Besides, I see no need to encourage you to hunt down some half-dressed strumpet. They seem to find you just fine all on their own."

Their carriage pulled up to their hotel and they quickly climbed up to their suite. Kat was relieved to see that it was not in complete disarray, although the maid could have been a little more meticulous in her cleaning. Their muddy clothes still formed a soggy pile in a corner of the bathroom and most of the furniture had merely been turned upright and not moved back into proper order.

Jerry tucked away the watch in a small air vent cut into the wall near the fireplace. There was a lip just inside the vent hole and both watches fit quite nicely inside. If you didn't know just where to feel around, you'd have a hard time putting your hand on them.

"I've seen better hiding places, Jerry. You don't need a college education to spot a vent hole in a wall."

"They've already searched our room, Kat. It's human nature not to come back and do it again, but even if they do, this is still a good spot. You won't find anything there unless you've got plenty of time to conduct a very thorough search. I'm betting that won't be the case."

"I hope you're right, Jerry.

"Say, I'm taking a bath, hon, I need to release my boobs from this so-called dress. I feel like I've been wrestling with a boa constrictor all day.

"Um, why don't you join me?" she added coyly, hoping the olive branch of her naked body in their shared tub would soothe Jerry's bruised ego.

Jerry smiled up at her, fully aware of what she was doing.

"Okay, babe, I'm sorry I've been acting like such a dick. I just hate it when you keep me in the dark like that," he murmured, giving her a warm hug and nuzzling into her neck. "How am I supposed to keep you safe if you don't keep me in the loop?"

"Maybe you could let *me* keep *you* safe for a change, Jer," Kat whispered back.

Jerry snorted and said, "Right. Let me know when that's the plan so I can get my will in order."

"Oooh, *bad move*, buddy. I think I just ran out of extra room in my tub!" and giggling, she scampered into the bathroom, with Jerry following hot on her heels.

"IT'S STILL NOT a sure thing we can find her," said Jerry, lolling back in the tub and piling up a little pyramid of soap bubbles on his chest.

"I dunno, Jer. I got a good look at the wagon she was riding in this morning on her way to Tourney. There can't be that many 'Purveyors of Mystical Crystals and Healing Stones" in one village. It's too bad there's no local directory my Slimlines can link into, but I'll bet the front desk guy can point us in the right direction."

"And what are you going to say to her when you find her?" asked Jerry suspiciously. "You weren't exactly the picture of warm hospitality the first time we met her."

"Well, I'm assuming that she'll actually be wearing real clothes this time and not some slip of red tissue that she's falling out of – and onto you.

"And I don't think we'll have to say much, anyways. I have a feeling once you wave that watch in front of her face she'll sing like Maria Callas."

Jerry chuckled. Five more years with him and Kat would end up sounding like a 20th century refugee fresh out of a time machine.

Jerry started working on building another little pyramid when he heard a murmur from Kat.

"Hmm, that's interesting…" Kat muttered quietly, eyes flickering behind her Slimlines.

"What's up, Kat?"

"Oh, I'm just reading up about those poor creatures they were torturing in the arena this morning."

"Wha? I thought you don't have any network access."

"Don't need it, Jer. Remember, these things have 640 exabytes of storage. Every day on their own they download hundreds of terabytes of recent scientific papers, news reports, instructional videos, that sort of thing. If they keep doing that, my internal storage should max out in about… oh, somewhere around two thousand years from now.

"In the meantime, there's precious little that's available on the net that I don't have at least a good chunk of already in storage."

"Holy crap."

"You said it, Jer, but listen to what I've learned about these animals – they're called 'Goddaffulls'."

"That's a strange name."

"I think it's a contraction of 'God Awfuls', which is what the original settlers thought when they first encountered them. They're the reason the Western continent has never been settled. They're not found on this continent at all. Traders have to cart them across the great central ocean from their native environment.

"And let me tell you, that Zimmerman guy wasn't just blowing bubbles. These are truly vicious beasts. They also have incredibly strong parenting instincts and will even sacrifice themselves to save their young. They're remarkably fecund, too – they make rabbits look like harem eunuchs. Each mating pair can produce as many as sixty offspring per year, for forty years in a row."

"My God, there must be millions of them on their continent!"

"Nature doesn't work that way, Jer. Where they live there's an even more vicious predator for whom Goddaffulls are the only choice for breakfast, lunch and dinner. These other beasts keep the population in check, and if it weren't for that prolific reproduction rate the species would have been wiped out long ago.

"Now here's the crazy part: about six years ago a team of exozoölogists actually went and *lived* with a herd of Goddaffulls!"

"Yeah, scientists do some crazy shit sometimes. What did they find out?"

"I dunno, I haven't gotten that far in the article yet, but there's also videos of them interacting with the creatures, and the first chance I get I'm going to watch that horror show. It's probably terrifying."

After they got out of the tub Kat said to Jerry, "I refuse to put on another one of those harlot outfits, Jerry. I'm invoking executive privilege and appropriating some of your garments. Like this doublet and breeches.

"Besides, I need to hide away my Slimlines while we're passing through public areas – I noticed at least a couple of very suspicious glances this morning and I'm terrified someone will figure out there's more to them than meets the eye, so to speak.

"It's almost impossible to tuck them out of sight when I'm cinched up in one of those medieval straightjackets women around here wear – there isn't room for so much as a coin to be wedged underneath or between my breasts. But the seamstress gave me several chest bands to be worn sort of like a primitive bra underneath a tunic – I can slide my glasses under the band and they'll stay safely in place beneath my boobs. If I wear a silk tunic under your leather doublet, I can keep my glasses completely invisible, but readily accessible, too.

"In fact…" she continued, "If I fold the bottom of the band up just so… I can make a little pocket. I can tuck in some mad money while I'm at it. Give me a couple of your coins, Jerry. A girl never knows when she might need to catch a cab."

Chuckling, Jerry tossed her some of his local currency. Kat fiddled around for a minute and said, "There! My own personal money belt!

"And if anyone has a problem with my fashion choices they can take it up with my boot. Just because men are obviously the ones who wrote the clothing rules, that's no reason to let myself be reduced to just a pair of tits and a pretty face and— NO, Jerry, don't say it if you know what's good for you."

Jerry's mouth snapped shut before he could utter a syllable. at was right – some things were better-left unsaid.

THE HOTELIER RAISED his eyebrows a bit when he saw Kat's outfit, but he'd been around long enough to know better than to make unsolicited comments. Besides, it hardly qualified as the strangest garb he'd seen in his years running a hotel. In response to their query he assured them that there were, in fact, no fewer than seven mystics in the village, and all used crystals in their healing.

"They are all well-known to the coachmen. But mayhap the hour is a tad advanced for such a visit," he added hesitantly. "Perhaps if you were to wait until tomorrow morning...."

"Of course," said Kat. "Perhaps just a relaxing tour in the night air, my love?" she said to Jerry. And thanking the Innkeeper, they slipped out onto the street.

They waved over a carriage that was sitting idle a few meters distant, and as they climbed in, Jerry said loudly, "Just a circuit around town, my man, we wish to take in the sights."

"At night, Milord?" asked the coachman, but shrugging his shoulders, he clucked the horse into action and they clip-clopped away down the cobblestone street.

If Kat had been wearing her Slimlines they might have alerted her to the pair of eyes hidden in the shadows partway down the street that watched her and Jerry get into the carriage.

Once they were out of sight and earshot of the Coughing Cat, Jerry tapped on the carriage roof. When it slowed he leaned out and said, "We seek a healer. But we aren't sure which," and he described the wagon that Kat had seen that morning.

Immediately the coachman said, "I know the establishment well, but I fear the hour is too advanced.

Perchance I could convey you tomorrow morn?"

"Of course, exactly my thoughts, but would you mind driving us past anyways, just so we can confirm it is the healer we seek?"

As they drove past, the healer's wagon was clearly visible sitting beside a large barn. Kat nodded at Jerry and they sat back and let the coachman drive them around for another half hour before exiting at the Coughing Cat.

This time, as the carriage moved off down the street after depositing Jerry and Kat at their hotel, the pair of eyes emerged from the shadows. They were attached to a large, heavy-set man wearing a long brown leather trench coat, and he quickly trotted up to the carriage and climbed inside. He called out a destination, and the carriage lurched back into motion and bore him away into the darkness.

ERRY AND KAT noisily reentered the inn and tottered drunkenly over to the hotelier.

"My good man," slurred Jerry, "We wish not to be disturbed for the rest of the night. Please make sure of that, won't you?" and he laid a gold coin on the podium by the book of reservations.

The Innkeeper's eyes bulged at the sight of the coin but he kept his composure and heartly assured Jerry, "Of course Milord. Fear not, I shall turn back even the hounds of Hell, should they come seeking you."

Jerry and Kat guffawed heartily, then staggered off towards their room and loudly clumped up the stairs. Thirty seconds later, in a considerably less boisterous manner, they descended the back stairs, slipped discreetly out the patio door and crept back up to the street through the slim gap on the building's north side.

"Are you sure you remember the way, Jer?"

Jerry tapped his temple with his index finger.

"In the vault, Kat. No magic glasses necessary."

Kat rolled her eyes then trotted along behind Jerry as they slipped through the dark deserted streets.

Well, there's one point for the old man's scorecard, she thought, as fifteen minutes later they turned a corner and saw the Mystic's house just a stone's throw away.

"How do you think we should play this?" Jerry whispered as they stood silently in the shadows peering closely at the house.

"I think the direct approach will work best here, Jerry. Follow me."

Kat strode up to the front door and started tapping frantically on the door. She kept it up for almost two full minutes until finally a sliver of light appeared around the door jamb.

"Go away! Have you lost your mind? We're closed! Off with you!" The voice was a woman's and Kat grinned evilly at Jerry.

"Please, mum, we need your elp!" she cried out in a squeaky falsetto. "It's me da', mum, e's got the pox or sumfin! E's all blue-like, mum! Oi fink e's dyin'! Please mum, we just need a moment o yur toim!" And she kept frantically tapping away.

The sound of a heavy bolt being slid back across the door scraped out at them, and the door opened a tiny crack.

"I ca—" was the most the woman got out of her mouth before Kat threw her shoulder at the door and sent it wobbling open, knocking the woman off her feet and sending her sprawling backward.

Kat and Jerry slipped inside, slammed the door shut behind them and threw the bolt.

It was the same woman, alright. The red dress had been replaced by an ankle-length linen nightgown and the lipstick and nail polish were gone, but there was no mistaking the same pair of big brown eyes and long raven-coloured hair around an almond-shaped face.

"It's – it's *you!*" whispered the woman, horrified. "How did you – what are you doing here? What do you want with me?"

"We want answers, that's what, lady. You can start with who you are and what your role is in this nonsense, and then we can move on to more weighty matters," snarled Kat.

"Easy, Kat, let's give the poor girl a chance to gather her thoughts."

"*'Poor gir'*—?!" started Kat, but Jerry waved her off.

"Miss," he said, "Take our word for it, we're not here to hurt you. We're just looking for answers, that's all. Can we sit down for a moment and explain everything over a cup of tea or something, and sort all this out?"

The woman nodded silently, but still kept her eyes on Kat, who hovered menacingly over her like an avenging angel waiting to deliver divine retribution.

Jerry helped her to her feet and picked up the lantern she'd dropped on the floor during Kat's entrance, before they headed to the back of the little house.

Sitting around an oval table five minutes later and nursing three cups of steaming liquid, the trio exchanged wary glances. Jerry was the first to speak.

"Ever since you approached us in that restaurant our lives have been in constant jeopardy, miss. My lady-friend here was almost murdered in the bathroom on the Space Elevator. We've been shot at and a friend of ours was impaled by an arrow, and our hotel room was all but demolished in a very thorough search.

"Now, before you say anything, I can tell you that we've pieced-together most of what is going on here. We know that the watch you were after contained information about a smuggling operation on this planet, and we've managed to decipher the data. We know everything right now except for the exact means the crooks are using to evade the export controls."

"You, you've read the disk?" she said, sounding astounded.

"Yes, and we've made multiple copies of the data, as well, so there's no point in trying to trick us out of it if you're worried about the information becoming public. The cat, for all intents and purposes, is well and truly out of the bag.

"But we still need to know how it's being done, and I think you can shed some light on that little conundrum.

"And I'd really like to know who you are," interjected Kat. "You sure as hell aren't some medieval necromancer hawking shards of cut glass and snake oil to the locals for a living."

"Oh, right. Sorry. You're right. I should introduce myself properly." Drawing herself upright and affecting an air of professionalism, she announced herself firmly: "Juanita Falcòn, Senior Investigator, Enforcement Division, GSC." And she stuck out her hand and shook Jerry's forcefully. Kat she merely smiled at meekly.

"What the hell is the 'GSC'?" asked Kat.

"Oh, sorry – 'Galactic Sporting Consortium'.

"We've suspected for a few years now that there was a smuggling operation moving large amounts of Aggresso – that's the drug they—" she began, but stopped when she saw Kat and Jerry's expressions.

"Oh, right. You probably already know all about that. Well, as I was saying, we've been on the trail of the smugglers for a while now and my contact – the man who died on the space station yesterday – my contact was supposed to pass me a watch containing a data disk that details the whole operation.

"He got it from a disgruntled member of the planet's Ruling Council who downloaded the information from a secure server kept offworld by King Sigismund's Royal Accountants.

"And judging by what you've already told me, the data is indeed there. But I can't believe you were able to find it. My contact had already hired computer experts offworld, without success. Even after disassembling the watch they still came up empty. He was meeting me to hand it over in the hopes we'd have better luck, but his cover must have been blown.

"And then we completely lost track of it. When we retrieved his body, the watch was gone. As were both of you. We couldn't even find you anywhere in the video surveillance records. It was as though you were just a figment of my imagination."

Kat smiled smugly and prodded Jerry in the side with her elbow.

"By the way, when this is all over, we'd sure like it if you could tell us how you did that. We don't like holes in our security system. And now I'd appreciate you telling me exactly who *you* are."

"No one but a couple of innocent bystanders pulled into a mess against their will, Juanita. But you can call me Jerry, and this is my main squeeze –" he chuckled at his appropriation of Melvin's phrase – "and you can call her Kat."

He did his best to ignore the evil eye Kat shot him, but shuddered as he caught a brief glimpse of it in the corner of his vision.

"Well, you've sure handled yourselves nicely for just a couple of innocent tourists who accidentally stumbled into an interplanetary conspiracy," said Juanita, "But the important thing now is getting that data off-planet. Do you still have the watch?"

"Yup, I brought it along. Here."

Jerry reached down into his jerkin pocket and pulled out the watch, then uttered a small curse. "Oh crap! I grabbed the wrong watch! This is *my* watch again! Dammit!"

Juanita looked devastated but Kat perked up immediately and said, "But the watch isn't even important anymore, Juanita – we have a copy of the data with us!"

"How?"

"I'm carrying a small computer with me. If you have a storage device I can transfer the data to it right away."

"No computer or storage devices here, but I can do you one better," said Juanita. Moving over to a tall glass hutch, she performed a series of little movements with some pegs sticking out of the wall. Silently, the hutch swung aside to reveal a large electronics array peppered with several small blinking lights.

"This is our planetside safe house, and every morning at 5 am local time a tight-beam communications signal is active from the ground station for exactly ten seconds. That's enough time to exchange any burst transmissions in either direction, but not long enough for the planetary monitoring stations to detect the signal.

"If you come back here tomorrow morning before 5 am we can transmit the data to my people on the Space Station. I wish you could tell me how they're managing to smuggle product off the planet, though. I was hoping that information was on the disk as well, but I guess that's not the case."

"Aren't you taking a big risk keeping that setup onsite?" asked Jerry. "I understand the penalties for such equipment are pretty severe."

"We have no choice. I can't exactly drop in to the station every time I need to talk to my unit – it's too risky. I don't want to blow my cover here.

"Which reminds me – how did you get here tonight? You didn't take any local transportation, did you?"

"No, we drove by earlier in a carriage but we didn't stop. We came back on our own afterwards."

"Good. You can't be too careful. This is an ugly business and I'm sure it's already left a long trail of bodies behind it."

Jerry and Kat promised to be back at 4:30 in the morning, a prospect which made Kat's entire body recoil, and then slipped out onto the dark street and headed to their hotel.

"Let's take a roundabout route back, Kat. I don't want any prying eyes piecing together our path."

They cut away several streets to their left, then turned back toward the general direction of the Coughing Cat.

"This is eerie, Jerry. I think we went too far off the beaten path. This quadrant is virtually deserted."

About fifteen minutes later, padding silently along the dirt road, they came in sight of a carriage parked in the shadows, far off to the east, just past a small copse of trees.

"That seems like a strange place to park," muttered Jerry. "There's no dwellings or other buildings anywhere in sight. Maybe the driver is grabbing a nap before the pubs close and business picks up again."

"Jerry…."

"What is it, Kat?"

"Jerry, can you see the right rear corner of the carriage from here?"

"Yeah… why?"

"You see that broken corner at the top, as though the carriage had been backed into a tree or a building once?"

"Yes...."

"Jerry, that's the carriage you and I took earlier. I recognise that damage."

They looked at each other in terror, and then Jerry said, "What do you think? Go over and check it out or run like hell?"

"I think we need to check it out."

"Okay, Kat, I hope your instinct is right."

Creeping stealthily through the shadows up to the carriage, Jerry slid along the right side of the wagon while Kat crept along the left. When he drew even with the little side window in the carriage door Jerry shot a glance into the carriage but it was empty inside. He saw Kat looking in through the opposite window and he shook his head, then moved forward towards the driver's bench up front.

The driver was there. Lying down on the bench, but not sleeping. A thick puddle of blood dripped from his neck onto the bench and spilled in a little stream onto the ground beneath. His face was frozen in a rictus of pain, and his fingers were bent and twisted into a horrific position. Two of them had evidently been sawed-off, and Jerry spotted one laying in the pool of blood on the ground.

Kat came around the corner and eyed the scene with a silent little gasp, then her eyes met Jerry's and they both said at once: "Juanita!"

If they'd thought about it, they probably would have taken the carriage back to Juanita's house but in their panic they simply turned on their heels and took off like demons, running at top speed through the deserted streets back to the safe house.

WITCH

They were still a few minutes away when they saw the orange glow that lit up the sky in the direction they were running. When they finally arrived they joined a small group of a dozen onlookers who had been drawn out of their houses by the sight of the blaze.

The whole house was engulfed in flames by now. A few members of the local fire brigade had formed a bucket line and futilely threw little splashes of water on the conflagration.

Hanging by the neck from a thick branch of a tree in the front yard was Juanita's lifeless body, swinging gently in the roiled air currents streaming away from the house. On her chest, painted in thick red ink across her white nightgown, was the word "WITCH".

14

S THEY STUMBLED through the dark streets back to their hotel Kat was verging on the hysterical.

"We killed that woman, Jerry! How could we have been so careless!"

"Calm down, Kat. One, we weren't careless – we were plenty careful to cover our tracks. And two, before we had a chance to talk with her we had no clue what side she was on. She could easily have been part of the group that's been trying to kill us all this time. She had a dangerous job and it caught up with her. That doesn't make what happened okay, but I wouldn't go so far as to say we're responsible for her death.

"In fact, Kat, I think we should count ourselves lucky we weren't caught in the crossfire – it's possible her attackers missed us only by a matter of minutes. She probably opened the door to them thinking it was us."

"Maybe you're right, Jerry, but I still feel like shit. And now I'm scared we're firmly in the crosshairs again. Aren't you?"

…?

"Jerry?" said Kat, turning around to see what he was up to in the dark.

The canvas hood came down over Kat's head before she could complete her turn, and as she flung her arms up to grab at the bag over her face, she felt a massive smack on the back of her head. She went limp as her world crumpled into a tiny little dot, and then was snuffed out completely.

IT WAS THE ROAR of the crowd that woke Kat up.

As her mind slowly climbed back up out of the pitch-black well it had fallen into, she heard the cheers and bloodthirsty cries. The roar was like a battering ram hammering away at her head. It hurt even to flicker her eyelids, but she knew she had to open her eyes eventually. Bit by bit, she forced them open as she struggled to make sense of the swirling mass of colours that spun in her vision.

She was in a cage. Lying in the back of an open wagon. In the middle of the arena.

Clawing to her feet in terror, Kat looked around her but all she could see was the crowd, frenzied, screaming, hysterical faces twisted with bloodlust and excitement.

Most of her clothing had been removed and all that remained was the tunic she had worn underneath the doublet. A frantic thought occurred to her and she anxiously patted at her chest and then breathed a huge sigh of relief. Her chest band was still in place and she could feel the telltale shape of her glasses, still snugly nestled against her skin beneath her breasts.

But right now there were more urgent matters to attend to.

She looked to her left and spotted Jerry in his own cage, clad only in a loincloth, not five meters away. He was moving slightly, but the roar of the crowd hadn't quite woken him up yet.

"Jerry!" she screamed, trying to raise her voice above the cacophonous howling filling the arena.

"Jerry! Wake up, Jer! Jerry!"

Slowly, Jerry lifted his head, then snapped around and saw Kat in her cage. Immediately, he understood what was happening.

"Kat! Are you okay? Are you hurt?"

"I'm okay, Jerry, but that might be changing real soon," and she gestured to the far end of the arena where three Goddaffulls were being herded in by several large men wielding sharp pikes.

"Hey!" Jerry screamed at the crowd, leaping to his feet. "Hey! This is a mistake! Let us out! Someone is trying to kill us!"

The crowd roared in approval at his cries for assistance.

"Let us out! This isn't right!" screamed Kat, and the roars increased in intensity. The spectators were exulting in the show, and cheering nonstop.

Two large men wearing vests of chain mail armour came over to Kat's cage and yanked at the latch, then opened the gate. One of them reached a huge meaty fist in and grabbed a handful of her hair. He tugged her forward and threw her onto the ground. She looked to her left and saw Jerry being yanked out of his own cage. The wagons pulled away and the armour-clad men trotted away after them, leaving Kat and Jerry completely alone in the middle of the arena, except of course for the three Goddaffulls that had caught their scent and were now pawing their way over to them.

Kat shrieked in terror and the crowd roared back. Jerry ran over and helped her to her feet, and the crowd roared louder still. The howls seemed to irritate the three beasts and they came closer, snorting and emitting loud grunts of anger. They swept the air with their razor-sharp tusks and stamped on the ground.

"My God, Jerry, what are we going to do? These creatures are going to tear us limb from limb and the crowd will only cheer louder!"

"Hold on, Kat, I'm thinking – maybe we can vault over the arena walls into the crowd."

But a quick glance to the side immediately disabused him of that notion; a line of heavily armed guards stood just inside the arena walls.

One of the beasts had gotten close enough to strike them, and viciously thrust out its head, almost impaling Jerry on one of its tusks. Kat and Jerry stumbled backwards but noticed that another of the beasts was moving around to their left side, while the third headed to their right.

"They're trying to surround us, Jerry!"

Jerry looked around frantically, but there was nothing in sight that could assist him. The swinging heads slashed the air with huge sweeps of their deadly tusks. Jerry realised they had only minutes before the two of them would be hemmed in and gored to death. There was no escape.

The roar of the crowd was shaking the walls of the arena as the spectators' screaming rose to a fever pitch. The crowd could sense the imminent slaughter and it drove them to the brink of madness.

Jerry looked over at Kat and was astounded to see her pulling out her Slimlines and putting them on.

"Kat!" he screamed over the crowd, "What in the world are you doing?"

"I'm going to watch that video the exozoölogists made! The ones who lived with these creatures! See if you can keep the beasts distracted for a minute while I play it!"

Keep the beasts distracted?! Does she think I have a pocketful of fireworks, maybe?

"Play tagged Goddaffull video!" Kat screamed at her Slimlines. Immediately, a series of title bars started to scroll across her vision while a monotone voiceover droned out, *"Goddaffulls, the terror of Planet Camelot. Watch with us as a team of brave exozoölogists actually moves in with a herd—"*

"Skip intro!" screamed Kat. "Play at double – no, triple speed!"

Jerry, meanwhile, had his hands full with the Goddaffulls, but had accidentally discovered that if he moved in close enough, he could grab onto the base of a tusk and keep from being gored, and at the same time prevent being trampled.

He was presently being dragged and tossed across the dirt as the Goddaffull he clung to howled viciously in frustration and flung its head from side to side in an attempt to dislodge its unwelcome occupant.

One of the other Goddaffulls lurched forward in an attempt to gore Jerry with its own tusk, but in the process inadvertently sliced a deep gash in Jerry's beast, and a stream of bright yellow fluid gushed out of its flank.

The wounded beast staggered backwards into the third creature, who snorted and kicked a vicious blow of its own at the offending animal's other flank. This caused it to careen back in the other direction, once again towards the bloodied tusks of the other Goddaffull.

Jerry was wondering how long he could keep this up when he glanced over at Kat and to his astonishment saw her ripping off her tunic and standing stark naked in the arena.

At this, the crowd howled in delight, and started screaming obscene epithets. Kat ignored them all and instead dropped to her knees and buried her face in the dirt. Thrusting her arms straight out above her head, she craned her head back and started screeching at the top of her lungs, "SQUEEEE! SQUEEEE! SQUEEEE!"

Jerry briefly wondered if the terrifying event had caused her mind to snap, when she looked up at him and screamed, "Jerry! Let go and get down on the ground! Do what I'm doing!"

And once again she craned her neck back, thrust out her arms and screeched, "SQUEEE! SQUEEE! SQUEEE!"

Figuring this was as good a way to die as any other, Jerry decided to follow Kat's instructions. At an opportune moment he released his hold on the Goddaffull's tusk and rolled away a couple of meters, where he then fell face-first onto the ground and thrust out his arms, yelling, "SCREEE SCREEE SCREEE!"

No, Jerry," came Kat's voice. "You're doing it wrong! Not 'SCREEE' – *'SQUEEE'*, Jerry, *'SQUEEE'!*"

"SQUEEE!" he screeched, "SQUEEE! SQUEEE!"

"SQUEEE!" screeched Kat.

"SQUEEE!" echoed Jerry.

It's not working, thought Jerry. Whatever trick Kat thought she had up her sleeve, the creatures were still headed right at both of them.

The wounded beast was the first to make it over to where Jerry knelt in the dirt, still screeching pathetic "Squeee"s at it.

Jerry saw it lower its head to gore him and he closed his eyes in terror. The crowd shrieked and howled as the tusks descended to strike the killing blow.

Jerry felt the *swish* of the creature's tusks as they sliced through the air above his head, and then choked in shock as a huge, warm viscous glop of foul-smelling green ooze burst from the Goddaffull's snout and almost completely engulfed his cowering form.

He looked over at Kat and she, too, had been coated with green ooze by the beast towering above her. But much to his amazement, it was now gently nuzzling its snout up against her. Its thick tongue extended from its jaws and scraped heavily over her body where she lay.

Jerry felt the same rough sensation, as his beast's sandpapery tongue scraped back and forth across his back, only to drench him again with more green ooze, which it then proceeded to mop up off him.

"They think we're baby Goddaffulls, Jerry," came Kat's voice as she writhed beneath the scaly tongue scraping her back.

"That's why I had to remove my tunic – when these things are babies they're all soft and pink and their parents do this to them to stimulate the growth of their scaly armour. They're so blinded by the sun we're only hazy shapes to them, but our general silhouette matches their offspring's, along with our cries!"

When the screaming spectators first saw the Goddaffulls clustered around Jerry and Kat, they thought the creatures were stomping them or bashing them with their snouts, and their bloodthirsty cries had crescendoed in volume. But as it became clear that the beasts were no longer filled with murderous fury, the shouting and cheering died almost completely away, and an eerie silence descended over the crowd. Suddenly, then, from one of the cheap seats in the upper level, came the shout, "WITCH!"

The onlookers couldn't understand what was happening, and came to the conclusion that Kat and Jerry had somehow bewitched the animals with evil black magic.

"WITCH! WITCH!" The cries were coming more rapidly now, from all over the arena. Some of the people in the rows closer to the center began throwing various food items. The guards looked confused and hesitantly began to move forward, lowering their pikes and tentatively approaching the group.

"Jerry! Grab the latch on the side of the harness, just below its ear, and pull!"

Jerry reached up and tugged the latch, and with a metallic *clack* it snapped open and fell to the ground beneath the animal. He spun to his left and repeated the action with the second of the huge brutes, just as one of the guards decided the time had come to attack Jerry, in the hopes of ending the debacle.

The guard thrust his pike forward but missed him as Jerry twisted to the side to avoid the blow. But before the man could lift his pike to try again, the animal towering over Jerry concluded that this poor helpless infant was being threatened. With an ear-shattering roar it spun like lightning and drove its center tusk directly through the guard's sternum, then jerked its head upright and sent the guard's body flying through the air.

Now that the harnesses were off, the Goddaffulls no longer shuffled and stumbled. They moved with a speed that was breathtaking to behold, spinning and stomping and goring every guard in sight.

The guards ran in terror across the sandy pitch of the stadium and the Goddaffulls thundered after them, leaping onto the men's backs, crushing spines and disemboweling them with their blood-covered tusks.

One guard made the ill-advised choice of scrambling over the arena wall to escape through the stands, but this just inspired the Goddaffull to leap in after him, where it then proceeded to rampage through the crowd, which was no longer cheering in bloodlust but rather screaming in abject terror.

The two other beasts followed suit, and within minutes thousands of shrieking audience members were running for their lives, themselves trampling young and old alike in a desperate attempt to find an exit before being crushed by the rampaging beasts.

Kat grabbed her tunic off the ground and ran, still stark naked, toward a barred gate in the arena wall.

"This way, Jerry," she shouted as she struggled to pull the tunic over herself. They ran through the arch and were confronted by a huge cage, where at least a dozen other Goddaffulls milled about. The smells and sounds coming from the arena had driven the animals inside the pen into a frenzy, but they were all tightly shackled by their harnesses and could do little more than groan painfully in the dark.

Kat pulled up the latch on the gate and swung it open. Running directly into the pen, she proceeded to move from animal to animal, snapping free their harnesses.

"Hey!" came a shout from the other side of the cage, where it opened into the passageways beneath the arena. "Hey, stop that!"

Not considering the consequences of what he was doing, the guard on the other side of the cage wall opened the grate and rushed inside to grab Kat before she could unharness any more of the beasts. He didn't make it farther than three steps in before a gigantic tusk impaled him from behind and flung him against the stone wall of the passageway.

"They still think we're their babies, Jer! We smell like them from all that green slime they dumped on us! Come this way – we can get out through this passageway!"

Jerry was busy releasing the last of the harnesses, and he watched in awe as the entire enraged herd of monsters stampeded through the dark passageway and into the corridors running beneath the arena. Within a few heartbeats the sounds of shrieking noticeably increased in volume, as the newly-freed animals tore through the stadium levels, devouring and dismembering every human they came across.

Before she dove into the dark tunnel leading away into the stadium, Kat turned around to assess the carnage in the stands. The King was lying splayed out on his back in the Royal Box, as a thick river of blood poured from a ragged hole in his chest. The Queen was about ten feet away, her skull crushed to pulp, sprawled face-down beside a little gold tiara that was flattened into a twisted ribbon.

The Goddaffulls were still raging through the mass of people jammed-up in the bleachers. One beast was thundering straight at a fat man of about sixty and a younger, buxom blonde woman beside him who were scrambling toward an exit stair. Just before Kat turned away, she saw the creature lift the man up into the air with its center tusk, and fling him viciously into the stadium wall.

Happy Tourney, Melvin Zimmerman, thought Kat, and she spun in a circle and raced into the darkness after Jerry.

**HE SCENE** in the pageant field outside
the arena was no less apocalyptic, as several
of the Goddaffulls were rampaging
through the assembled vendor wagons and
food carts. Tourney spectators who had
managed to escape the arena were now fleeing pell-mell across
the open space, but the Goddaffulls were cutting them down
with impressive efficiency, slashing and stomping and goring
and gouging the screaming masses with abandon. Long
months of torturous captivity were being repaid in savagery,
and the beasts' eyes glowed with blood madness stoked by the
many kills.

Kat and Jerry came upon a haberdasher's wagon upended
by one of the beasts. The proprietor lay face-down in the
muck, a huge puddle of red liquid slowly spreading out from
beneath him. Clothing was scattered across the ground and
spilling out of the wagon.

"Quick, grab some breeches and a tunic," said Kat, pulling
off her own soiled tunic and standing in the field stark naked
before pulling on a festival dress that lay gently fluttering in
the breeze on the side of the upended wagon.

Jerry tangentially mused on the thought that for probably
the first and only time, Kat could stand naked in broad
daylight surrounded by masses of people, and not a single soul
would be interested in looking her way. And to think only 24

hours earlier she'd been self-conscious about wearing a low-cut gown! He chuckled to himself, then grabbed a pair of leather boots he found partially covered by the wagon, and grunted in satisfaction to discover that they fit him very comfortably.

"Help me rip my old tunic in half," called Kat. "There's a lot of that green slime soaked into it – if we each tie a long strip of it around our waists it should be enough to keep us from becoming Goddaffull kibble."

Hundreds of dead or twitching bodies littered the pageant field. The cries coming from the stadium had all but disappeared, with only the odd shriek of terror or pain leaking out. More of the beasts emerged from the arena, blinking in the sun as they passed out of the darkness of the entrance tunnels.

To their left, one Goddaffull was emitting thunderous roars and the others gradually made their way in its direction.

"Jerry, I think that one is calling the others – it looks like the herd might be moving off into the forest now."

"Then it's a good time for us to make our escape – let's move."

Sprinting across the field, they dodged moaning bodies and flailing shapes clutching wounds or stumps of limbs, and ignored the pitiful cries for help as they made a beeline down the hillside back toward the town.

"That was excellent work back there, Kat – I didn't know what to think when I saw your naked butt sticking up in the air while you sucked up stadium dirt and screeched."

"We should send a donation to that team of exozoölogists. The video showed them doing the same thing to get accepted by the herd."

"Thank God for your Slimlines. We'd be nothing but partially digested Goddaffull meals right now if it weren't for those glasses."

"Still think I overpaid for them?" asked Kat, smiling wickedly.

They came to the bottom of the hill and turned down a street to their left, heading towards the Coughing Cat, with every intention of grabbing their things and making the world's fastest exit off the planet. But when they turned another corner, they came to a sudden stop as they found themselves hemmed in by a group of tall, heavy-set men, and, in the rear, several scowling thugs wearing long, dark brown leather trench coats.

Kat spun in a circle, but saw that another group of men had run up behind her and Jerry, boxing them in between the buildings.

A man carrying a long thick truncheon stepped forward slowly toward Jerry, who crouched in a defensive posture and readied himself to parry the attack.

The man was insanely fast, moving with superhuman speed as he launched himself forward, swinging the club at Jerry's head.

Kat watched, horrified, as the blow impacted solidly with Jerry's skull, lifting him up into the air with the force of its impact, accompanied by a sickening crunching sound.

Jerry was knocked backwards several feet and lay motionless, crumpled in a twisted heap.

Kat snarled and readied herself to launch a roundhouse kick at an attacker who was approaching her cautiously. Before the man could take another step toward her, though, she herself felt a punishing blow against her skull. The world spun in a crazy circle around her as she sank to the ground.

"Should I kill her now?" she heard a rough voice say just above her head.

"No, ignore her – she's worthless. He's the one we want. We need him to read that timepiece we took off him last night."

"But she's a witch. You heard what she did in the arena."

"I said leave her – those who didn't die today will do worse than you when they find her."

Through a slitted eyelid, Kat watched in a hazy sideways blur as one of the men grabbed Jerry by the ankle and dragged him face down through the muck before disappearing out of view.

The man who had struck Kat in the head launched a brutal series of vicious kicks to her stomach, grunting with malicious delight at hearing her groan in agony.

"That's for my uncle," he said quietly. "I saw his head ripped right off his body by one of those beasts you bewitched."

He launched another series of kicks, into her ribs this time, and Kat felt something inside her go *snap*!

"And that's for the King and Queen."

A final blow caught Kat on her shoulder and she felt a lance of pain shoot up her neck. "And that one's just for me. Whore."

His shadow briefly passed over her as he moved away to join his companions. Kat lay gasping in the mud, the taste of blood bitter in her mouth, as she slowly slipped into unconsciousness.

*   *   *

"MISS? MISS? Are ye awake, lassie? Cannae ye hear?"

Forcing her eyes open, Kat managed to make out the general outlines of an old man's face that exhibited an expression of concern as it hovered close above her own.

"Lassie, are ye dying? Where did the beastie get ye?"

Summoning superhuman strength from a reservoir she didn't know she possessed, Kat forced her arm down and into her dress, where she scratched at the band of fabric still wrapped around her just beneath her breasts. A moment later her hand emerged, clutching something small and round.

"Ay? Whass this?" the man asked, as Kat feebly reached out to him. Grasping his hand, she pressed into it a small wooden disk inscribed with a unique, unmistakable mark. Then, with a gasping sigh, she fell back down into that bottomless pit of blackness that she was getting to know so well.

16

TINY PINPRICK of light appeared in Jerry's vision, a micro-dot of illumination in the vast stygian darkness that engulfed him. Slowly, the dot began to widen and grow in intensity, until it became so bright Jerry tried to squint his eyes shut to block it out.

"He's waking up," he heard a voice say.

"About freakin' time," came a second, rougher voice. "I told those savage idiots downstairs we needed him. They came *this close* to killing the bastard. Morons."

A stretch of silence, then, as Jerry's mind continued its pilgrimage back into the land of the conscious.

"Can he talk?" came the rough voice again.

"Patience. Patience. We're lucky he still has a heartbeat. Talking might take a bit longer."

"We don't have 'longer'. We have only 'yesterday'. Give him some more of that stuff. Wake him up so he can talk."

"If I give him much more it might finish the job your associates started. If you really need information from him you'll just have to wait a bit longer."

Jerry heard a curse of anger, then the sound of heavy boots moving across a tile floor.

"Have it your way," said the rough voice again from farther away. "Get him conscious and call me when he can talk. And whatever you do, don't let the asshole die."

The sound of heavy boots tromping away down a hallway echoed through the room, and Jerry let their metronomic thumps chaperone him back into the land of darkness, as the spotlight in his mind dimmed and finally went out once again.

AT OPENED her eyes and peered at the room around her.

The pillow beneath her head felt soft and comfortable, and the blanket on top of her was warm and cozy. A row of candles flickered silently off to her side, and a fat orange cat sat on a low table a few feet away, studiously chewing on one of its paws while watching her with a beady-eyed stare.

A child who had been sitting near the foot of her bed jumped up and ran out of the room upon seeing that she was awake, and returned a moment later trailing a peasant woman and hiding behind her dress as she came over to Kat and leaned down to look at her face.

"I was wondering how long you would wait to rejoin us," said Mathilde, smiling at Kat. "For a while there, I thought we might lose you. From what I heard from a boy who was hiding nearby in the bushes, you took quite a beating. Many girls wouldn't have survived it. You're a tough little fighter, lass."

Kat gave Mathilde a weak smile and whispered, "Not my first rodeo, Mathilde, sad to say."

"Not your first what? – Oh, nevermind, lass. Lie still a moment and let me check your poultice," and she started poking around at a small mass of cloth wrapped around Kat's sternum. e

Kat started in shock as a thought occurred to her.

She frantically patted herself down and flung her head from side to side, searching the room desperately with her eyes.

"Here, here! What did I say about laying quietly? What's come over you, lass?"

"My glasses!" said Kat. "Have you seen my glasses? Did anyone bring back my glasses?"

"Your 'glasses'?" repeated Mathilde in a puzzled tone. "What are you— OH! Do you mean these spectacles, dear?" Reaching behind Kat's head, she picked up a pair of eyeglasses off the night table and held them out to Kat.

"Elric spotted them buried in the muck underneath your body when we went out to collect you."

"Oh, Mathilde! I was so scared! Oh, oh," and Kat broke down, weeping as the shock of her recent ordeals suddenly overwhelmed her.

"There, there, child, it's all right. You're safe now. You need rest. Get some more sleep – I'll bring you some soup in a bit, and you can start to regain your strength."

Such a fuss over a pair of spectacles, clucked Mathilde quietly to herself as she slipped back out of the room. *That poor girl is teetering on the edge of madness, I fear.*

WHEN SHE CAME BACK an hour later, Mathilde tsk-tsk'ed and reached for the glasses that Kat clutched in her hand as she slept, but when she tried to pry them from her grasp, Kat woke up with a look of panic on her face, and then sighed and relaxed back against the pillow, still firmly clenching the glasses.

"Well, there's nothing wrong with your grip, apparently," said Mathilde. "Do you think you can eat a bit of soup?"

Kat smiled and nodded and Mathilde called out to the other room. The child reappeared, carefully holding a bowl of soup in both hands, and slowly brought it over to Kat's bedside. Mathilde helped her sit up a bit in the bed and began to feed Kat spoonfuls of the steaming broth.

"I hear that was quite a show you put on in the arena, my dear," said Mathilde quietly as she ladled another helping of broth into Kat's mouth. "All the planet's talking about the Naked Witch who ensorcelled the Devil's Hounds."

"Who…? What…? You think that I—"

"Oh, hush, dear – your secret's safe with me, although I can't promise how long it will be before someone connects the woman beaten in the street with the Sorceress who destroyed the Tourney. That red hair of yours is a dead giveaway – there's not many comely young things like you with such a brightly-coloured mane."

"Were you there, in the arena? Did you see—"

"Who? Me? At the Tourney? Never even once, my dear! That savage barbarity has no place in any proper Christian, God-fearing land. I thank the Good Lord Himself for delivering us from that blight.

"Never would I have guessed that he would choose a slip of a girl like you as His Instrument, but the Lord works in mysterious ways, of course. *'And a child shall lead them'*," intoned Mathilde solemnly.

"I don't think I'm actually God's 'instrument'," said Kat, but Mathilde cut her off brusquely.

"Shush your mouth, child! It is not for us to question the ways of the Creator. You'd best stop those thoughts before you slip into blasphemy."

"Well, when it comes down to it, Mathilde, what did I really do? I disrupted the games for a bit, but I'm sure the wheels of commerce will start turning again in no time, and everything will return to its usual state."

"Oh lass, do you really not understand what you have wrought?

"A few years ago, the fools who run the Tourney thought they would provide the crowd with a bit of a thrill, and decided to present a 'special' fight with one of the creatures that was rotting away in the pens. The beast was old and crippled, and they decided to risk fighting it without the benefit of a restrictive harness. They ringed the arena with twenty of the King's best pikemen, and set the animal loose.

"It slaughtered all of them, in vicious, blood-soaked fury, and then escaped the arena and disappeared into the woods.

"For the next six months it terrorized the village, and in the process devoured hundreds of citizens and farm animals. When they were finally able to track the beast down and corner it, they needed almost a legion of the finest soldiers in the Realm to slaughter it. That was *one* old, crippled creature already at the end of its natural lifespan.

"You released no fewer than *twenty* of the creatures, all young and healthy, fertile and in their prime mating years. I have heard that some of them were already pregnant with their new litters ready to emerge.

"Right now, it's quiet. The beasts all ate well at the fairgrounds, and they're probably busy digging themselves a nest somewhere in the forest. But within a week they'll start to venture out into the countryside to feed, first on most of the livestock, then eventually in the villages.

"I suspect that before the new moon arrives, not a single human being will be left alive on this planet. Those not lucky enough to escape to different worlds will instead be lining the digestive tract of one beast or another."

"Oh my God," said Kat, hand to her mouth. "I never intended to—"

"Hush child, you've done a wonderful thing. This world was rotting from the inside out. The Lord has decided to wipe it clean, just as he did with Sodom and Gomorrah.

"Although…." and Mathilde paused for a moment.

"What?" said Kat.

"Well, child, did you really have to do it *naked?*"

ATHILDE WAS LIKE a mother hen, popping in every five minutes to check on Kat, fluffing her pillows, bringing her drinks or fussing with the bedclothes.

Kat was still feeling pretty groggy, and her sides screamed in pain whenever she tried to move or even sit up, but it was clear her recovery was gaining momentum.

"You know, dear, you've been sort of a personal blessing to me, too," said Mathilde shyly while she wiped Kat's face with a cool, wet cloth.

"What do you mean?"

"Well, you remember Elric, who brought you to town in his wagon?"

"Of course."

"Um, it's just that he and I… that is to say… we've been, ah, keeping company since then. You might say you brought us together, lass."

"Oh Mathilde! That's so wonderful! I'm so happy for you! He seemed like a very nice fellow."

"Aye, he is, lass. That he is…" and the woman blushed slightly.

"Well then, I see my work here is done," said Kat, smiling.

She drew herself upright and said, "Mathilde – I need to go! I can't lie here any longer. I need to go find Jerry. I think the men in brown trench coats took him. He's probably rotting in a dungeon somewhere. If he's still alive, that is," she added, in a fearful voice.

"If he is still alive, I doubt very much he's still on this planet," said Mathilde. "The men who attacked you are offworlders. That particular bunch are well known to us around here."

"But the trench coats! I thought—"

"Don't judge a wolf by its clothing, dear. They may dress the part but your assailants are just a gang of interlopers. They took your young man off-world, I can assure you of that. There's no telling where he is right now."

"Then that's even more reason I need to go now," said Kat forcefully, struggling to sit up and get her feet onto the floor.

Waving off Mathilde's hand, Kat stood up with great effort, but immediately lost her balance and sat down again hard.

"It's no use, child. You just don't have the strength yet. Now heed my advice and—"

"NO. I don't care how hard it is – I have to leave *now*."

Mathilde watched Kat struggle to her feet again, and pursing her lips in disapproval, said quietly, "I can see there'll be no stopping you." *Sigh*. "Hold on then a moment, lass, I might have something for you."

Mathilde disappeared into the other room and returned a minute later holding a small tin box in her hand. She pulled out a little chunk of brown fudge and handed it to Kat.

"Eat this," she said.

Kat looked skeptically at the little wedge and then slipped it into her mouth.

The effect was instantaneous. Kat's eyes brightened and cleared, she straightened her shoulders and stood upright, and stopped wobbling back and forth.

"What—"

"It's called 'Agresso', child. They use it in the arena. The men who attacked you probably took it before your encounter."

"Oh my God, it's amazing, Mathilde! I feel like I could run a marathon right now!"

"You probably could, dear, at least until it wears off. You should be good for the next few hours, though – long enough for you to get to the station and go find your young man."

Just at that moment the little child returned and tugged forcefully on Mathilde's dress.

"What is it dear?"

The child pointed at the front room and looked scared. "Men outside."

Mathilde looked alarmed and scurried over to the window, then quickly returned with a worried expression.

"It seems your presence here has not gone unnoticed," she said quietly. "A crowd is gathering. I heard the word 'witch'. You were right—you need to leave right away."

"I'm not leaving you here alone, Mathilde. I've seen what these mobs can do. If they think you're involved with me, they'll kill you and burn this house to the ground."

Kat shuddered.

"Any ideas?" she asked Mathilde.

Mathilde called the child over and said, "Go run fetch

Elric. Tell him to bring his wagon to the Church right away. Tell him to be quiet about it. And whatever happens, you stay with him. Don't you come back here for any reason. Use the back way, child. Now go!"

The youngster disappeared in a flash, running out the back door of the house and disappearing through a small gap in a hedge at the rear of the property.

Mathilde handed Kat the little tin containing the Agresso. "You might be needing this again, dear. I have no use for it."

She dumped a small pile of garments onto the bed and said, "Put those on quick, while I grab some of my belongings."

She bustled around, tossing a few knick-knacks and clothing items into a canvas carpetbag, then grabbed the surprised orange cat and stuffed it in as well, buckling the top over its head. Pausing in thought, she disappeared for a moment, then returned holding a small cloth bunny doll, opened the bag and stuffed it in alongside the annoyed-looking cat, then shut it again.

"Wouldn't do to leave behind Finnian," she said with a small smile. "I'd never hear the end of it."

"Let's hope the cat doesn't eat him," said Kat, then hustled over with Mathilde to the back door. Silently, they slipped into the back yard, trotted over to the hedge, squeezed into the gap, and ran across the field.

ELRIC WAS ALREADY WAITING at the Church when they got there, with a worried look on his face. A small bag sat on the wagon bench between him and the child.

"I twigged to what was happening," he said, nodding as he noticed Mathilde's carpetbag. "One good thing about poverty – not a lot to weigh you down."

"Blessed are the poor," said Kat.

"Amen, lass," replied Mathilde, squeezing onto the bench beside Elric while Kat and the child tucked themselves out of sight in the back of the open wagon. Kat recognised the smelly canvas tarp and shuddered, but nestled under it all the same.

"To the station, Elric, as fast as old Meggy can pull us."

"No!" called out Kat. "We need to go back to the Coughing Cat – I need to fetch some things."

"No time dear. You can buy new clothing when you're safely away from here."

"It's not clothing I'm after. Trust me, Mathilde, I have to go there."

Elric shrugged, then shook the reins and the wagon lurched away.

They got to the hotel without incident, and Kat raced upstairs past the startled Innkeeper and burst into her room. All their belongings were still in place. Either the hotelier was hoping to continue charging them for their suite, or the devastation that had descended on the village had emptied his establishment to where he didn't need to clean out the rooms with any urgency.

Kat dragged a chair over to the wall, stood on it and ferreted around in the vent hole for a moment, then pulled out two red cards on lanyards, two golden wristbands and the watch, along with a wad of credit notes. She stuffed them into a small handbag and then, as there was nothing else in the room that interested her, she raced back out into the street and leaped into the back of the wagon.

Her entry into the hotel had attracted attention, and already a small group of men were gathered around the wagon and muttering angrily. Kat saw several more men running down the hill towards them, calling out excitedly when they saw her. She reached into the handbag, pulled out the wad of credit notes and threw a bunch of them out into the street.

"Look!" she called out. "Money!"

Human nature being what it is, the crowd of men blocking the wagon's path forgot why they were there and leapt after the brightly coloured notes as they skittered across the cobblestones in the breeze.

"Go!" she hissed to Elric, but they were already underway.

Their pace wasn't going to break any speed records, though, and Kat could hear the thump of heavy footsteps running to catch up with them. A couple of heavy rocks whizzed past their heads, and then several more came flying at them from a side street, where some of their pursuers had detoured in an attempt to cut off their escape.

Mathilde leapt into the wagon bed, where she hunched over the child, sheltering it from the steadily increasing stream of projectiles.

Elric was shaking the reins frantically and whistling at Meggy, but the horse still barely trotted along.

"Can't this horse run any faster?" shouted Kat. "Why isn't Elric using the whip?"

"He doesn't carry one," answered Mathilde. "He hasn't the heart to whip the poor thing."

What Elric couldn't do, however, their attackers inadvertently accomplished for him. An especially heavy volley of rocks came at them, first from their right, and then from the opposite direction, as more men joined in the chase from both sides. Several of the rocks hit the horse, impacting with heavy thuds and leaving gashes in her hide, and one smacked her solidly in the muzzle just beneath her right eye, causing a thick stream of blood to gush out.

The frightened horse broke into a real gallop, nickering in pain and fear. Her timing was perfect, as at that very moment a large man had caught up with the wagon and was about to hoist himself into it over the side. The sudden increase in velocity caught him by surprise, though, and he lost his grip and tumbled backward onto the street.

Kat grabbed the edge of the canvas and held it at chest level to protect them from the barrage of rocks but still worried about a well-aimed impact against the horse's head. Another one like the first would probably bring her down.

Another burly man caught up with the wagon and climbed into it over the tailgate. He rose to his feet and faced them, brandishing a small short sword. His eyes gleamed evilly and Kat discerned the telltale signs of Agresso in his quickened movements.

They were moving at a much faster clip, now, and the canvas billowed out from Kat's grasp. She let it go and immediately it flew back and engulfed the man, who staggered backward. The vague outline of his shape showed he was struggling to pull the canvas free. Kat stepped up to him and, with a field-goal-worthy effort, launched a kick into his groin, clearly outlined against the flapping canvas.

An audible grunt of pain burst from the upper area of the canvas and the shape floundered backward into the tailgate, tumbled over and plunged to the ground, his head impacting with a sickening smack, and he lay motionless.

Most of the mob had been left far behind by now, but several drug-enhanced thugs remained in hot pursuit.

One threw himself at the side of the wagon and gripped onto the sideboard, trying to pull himself in. Kat batted at his

hands but his fingers were like little bands of iron wrapped around the sideboard rail. Shrugging, she leaned over, grabbed his head with both hands and then, with a mighty effort, twisted it savagely in a half circle. The sound of crunching bones and cartilage accompanied the man's fall, and his lifeless form tumbled away into a ditch.

Two more attackers hoisted themselves into the wagon but Kat had hit her stride now. The first one was on the receiving end of a whirling roundhouse kick to the face, shattering his jaw and launching him through the air and back to the road.

The second man was ready for her, but his drug-accelerated attack lacked the training and finesse of Kat's fighting skills. She easily ducked a looping right cross and deflected the left jab that followed, then proceeded to pummel the man with a withering array of blows to his head and body. The coup de grâce was a straight-arm thrust into his Adam's Apple, her knuckles crushing his trachea and knocking him off the cart.

With the coast finally clear, Kat sat down hard in the teetering wagon as it careened madly across the dried and hardened dirt road to the station.

Mathilde was staring at Kat in amazement.

"By the Holy Saints," she whispered, "is that what that drug does to you?"

"Well,' puffed Kat, brushing aside an errant strand of hair and leaning back in exhaustion, "that and daily jujitsu sparring with Jerry."

She smiled and said, "Maybe the next time we spar, I'll take just a teensy bit of this stuff – just to see his reaction, of course," and she giggled evilly.

"I never thought I'd be happy to be on a planet with no communications system," she said to Mathilde. "At least we don't have to worry about a reception party waiting for us when we reach the station."

As they drew near the east gate where she and Jerry had originally exited the station, Kat gave the red cards to Elric and Mathilde, who had moved back up to sit on the bench.

"Put these around your necks. Keep them with you at all times until you leave this planet. Now smile at the gate guard and show him the cards. You don't need to say a word."

The guard nodded when he saw the red cards but he stopped Kat, who held Mathilde's child on her lap.

"Offworlders or residents?" he asked.

"Offworlders."

"I'll need to see your passes."

Kat and the child raised their forearms to display the golden wristbands and the guard's eyebrows lifted a bit, but he just nodded and said, "Welcome back."

Elric drove the wagon forward and Kat pointed him over to the loading docks area.

As they pulled up, an attendant bustled over from a small glass-walled office overlooking the parking lot.

"Are you here to pick something up?" He frowned. "I don't have anything on my schedule. Because you can't park here. Loading and unloading only."

"Is there a stable or other area where you keep wagons and animals?" asked Kat.

"Of course," he replied. "How else would we make deliveries to the village?"

"Good," said Kat. She reached down into her handbag and extracted another thick sheaf of credit notes and held them out to him. "Because I want you to make it your personal mission in life to see to it that this wagon gets put in a safe berth and this horse gets the best care this station can offer."

The attendant's eyes widened into small saucers when he saw the bills but he said, "I can't. I mean, I *could,* but everything has to have the proper docs. I can't just wedge something in – the Chief Hostler would yank it out as soon as he saw it. Everything needs to be in the system."

Kat rolled her eyes, then said, "Hold on a sec," and she tapped her teeth together and her eyes flickered back and forth for a second behind her glasses, then she said, "There. Happy now?"

Confused, the attendant looked down at his tablet and said, "Wha— That wasn't there a minute ago!"

"But it's there now," said Kat.

"Now, are you going to take this money or do I have to drive over there myself and find someone who will?"

"NO MA'AM," said the attendant, stuffing Kat's credit notes down into a side pocket. Pulling a barcoded tag off a ring he carried on his belt, he attached it securely to the wagon rail and tapped away on his tablet.

They got down off the wagon and carried their bags over to the loading dock stair entrance. Elric hung back a moment and hugged his blood-spattered horse's neck tearfully, whispering into its ear. Then, reluctantly, he tore himself away and joined them at the stairs.

"Um, do you need directions?" the attendant called out.

"No thanks, I know the way," said Kat, and the little group filed through the doorway and disappeared out of sight.

NCE THEY WERE IN the main station concourse, Kat found a visitor's kiosk and asked the clerk, "Do you have a small, full-service boutique hotel in the station?"

"Of course. We have several."

"What's the best one?"

The clerk looked at Kat's shabby period clothing and hesitated, but when he noticed the intense "Don't-dick-with-me, asshole" look in Kat's eyes he quickly said, "That would be the *Prince Charibert,* located in quadrant eleven. It's a bit of a walk – I'll call you a shuttle."

Elric and Mathilde and the child had never ridden in an electric cart before, and as they zipped soundlessly through the concourse, all three clung tightly to the seat rails with a look of abject terror in their eyes. The lack of any visible driver also upset them no end. They were demonstrably relieved and leapt out of the cart upon arriving at the hotel.

Kat strode up to the reception desk and said, "What's your best available suite?"

A short, balding man wearing pince-nez glasses looked up sharply when he heard this and hustled over, elbowing away the other clerk.

"That would be our *Champs-Elysées* suite, mademoiselle, on our top floor."

"Are there any other suites on the same floor?"

"Ah, yes, just one other. The *Charlemagne.*"

"I'll take them both. Put the lady and the child in the *Champs-Elysées* – the gentleman gets the *Charlemagne.*"

"These people are my guests. They can stay as long as they want. Let's just block-out both suites for the next month, that should do for starters.

"I want you to treat them as though they are dying billionaires considering whether to put you in their will. They will receive your *personal* attention in every matter which concerns them."

The hotelier nodded quickly and gave Kat an obsequious smile that he hoped she would find reassuring.

"Does the hotel have a couturier?"

"Of course, mademoiselle, the finest—"

"Save the PR for the tourists. I don't have the time. Once they're settled-in, send up a tailor and a couturière. Take those rags they're wearing and burn them, then outfit them with enough clothing to last a month. *Modern* clothing – none of this Dark Ages shit. And luggage to keep it in. I'm partial to Louis Vuitton. Try to get some of that.

"Book them all full-day appointments in your spa and salon right away." Kat noticed the child scratching away at a spot on its neck. "Maybe even before they go to the room. Full makeovers for all of them, hair, skin, nails, the works. When I come back I want to be able to tell if that child is a girl or boy."

The little group was now staring goggle-eyed at a video playing on a wall panel to her left.

"They're going to need a bit of instruction. Send a maid or footman or someone up to the rooms with them for the first hour—" she watched as they *oohed* and *ahhed* and prodded each other excitedly at a scene in the video showing people relaxing beside a swimming pool. "Better make that two, no, three hours. Be sure to show them how to use the elevators and the phone. Have a tutor teach the child some basics. Maybe a tutor for all of them….

"They don't understand tipping. See to it that anyone who helps them out receives a generous gratuity – 20% at the very least. And never less than 20 credits for any service, even if it's just opening a door for them. I want every staff member of this hotel to compete to be their best friend."

At this point, it was all the hotel manager could do to keep from actually drooling. He jammed his fingernails into his palm in a desperate attempt to remain calm.

"What about food? Do you have room service?"

"Of course, mademoiselle, the fi—" He caught himself and said, "Um, anything in particular, or should I make a selection for them?"

"I'm going to trust your judgment on this one," said Kat. "Pretend you're a 14th century English serf who thinks Bangers and Mash is a delicacy."

The gentleman evinced a little shudder at the thought, which was horrifying to him on so many different levels, but said, "I shall provide them with fare which will send their tastebuds to heaven."

"Excellent. Three times a day. Don't make them come asking for it."

"My own dear departed mother, God rest her soul, would not get such attentive treatment from me, mademoiselle, were she still alive today. I shall treat your guests as royalty."

"You'd better, or when I come back you and I will have a very unpleasant conversation about it."

The hotelier smiled reassuringly. "You needn't be concerned."

"Good. Here. This is for you," and Kat placed a 10,000-credit note on the desk in front of him.

His gasp was audible, but the bill immediately vanished nonetheless, as he quickly passed his hand over the desk. He raised himself up on his tiptoes to keep from accidentally dancing in place.

Kat told her Slimlines to handle the payment and billing details with the hotel's computer, then turned to her friends and said, "I have to leave you now, but I'll be back. At least, I hope I'll be back. You can stay here at the hotel for as long as you want, but if I don't return sometime in the next, oh, three weeks, you can leave without me. There are literally hundreds of worlds you can choose from that will be happy to have you.

"This gentleman here," and she raised her voice slightly, to make sure he could hear her clearly, "will send up an interplanetary relocation specialist to meet with you to help you select the best fit for your needs. That person will get you passports and visas, too.

"The hotel will handle all the paperwork and payments for you, including any first-class transportation and resettlement expenses for wherever you choose, and will bill my account accordingly. Don't worry, they're happy to do it, especially since they'll be adding on a healthy service fee and commission for themselves.

"If there's anything else you see at the station that you want, have the merchant bill my account here. If anyone gives you a hard time, just tell this man and he'll fix it.

"Oh, I almost forgot," she said, turning back toward the manager at the desk, interrupting his ruminations on which elite colleges he would now be sending his children to. "There's a cat. Send up a veterinarian and a groomer to have it dewormed and to give it its shots and a flea bath. The lady will tell you what it likes to eat."

"Many of our patrons travel with their pets, mademoiselle. The cat will be no problem at all."

"Excellent, because I need to tell you there's also a horse."

"A… horse, mademoiselle?"

"Yes, a horse. I'm sure you've heard of them before. Like a cow, but skinnier."

The hotelier gave Kat a weak smile.

"It's here at the station stable. It's linked to my account in the system. See that a vet drops in on it, too, as well as a farrier. I want you to check on it daily. And be sure it doesn't accidentally end up on your menu – I'm wise to you Frenchies.

"It gets the royal treatment, too, or when I return you'll wish you could trade places with your mother."

And giving each of her dazed friends a warm hug, she ran back out to the station concourse, flagged down a shuttle, and disappeared into the distance.

AT'S FIRST STOP was Slaäm's office, and she sighed in relief to find him working at his desk.

"Kat! You're alive!" he exclaimed. "When I heard about what happened in the arena—"

Kat groaned. "Does *everyone* know about that?"

"Are you kidding? It's virtually the only thing people have been talking about for the last week. Although no one knows who the witch really is. I put it together immediately, of course, when I heard about the red hair and glasses."

He stopped talking for a moment and looked past her shoulder quizzically.

"Where's Jerry?"

Kat sank down into a chair in front of the desk and said, "That's why I'm here. They took Jerry. And a contact I have says they probably took him off-planet."

"OK, don't panic, then, Kat – if he left the planet he has to be in the system. There's no way around it."

Tapping at a monitor on his desk, Slaäm clicked around for a moment, frowning, and then grunted excitedly.

"Found him! But you're not going to like this."

"Hit me."

"Well, there's good news and bad news. The good news is, he's not left orbit. The bad news is that he's in the Detention Center."

"… Oh, and there's even worse news…" he added quietly, tapping away at the monitor again. "He's scheduled for a death match in the prison rec center in five days."

21

"**D**EATH MATCH?** What is *wrong* with this planet? Hasn't anyone here ever heard of tennis or baseball?"

"I hear you, Kat, but it's something the authorities let the penal facility get away with. The participants are all volunteers – or they're supposed to be, anyways – and it's another nice revenue stream for the planet. They hold them every week. Broadcast on pay-per-view.

"Jerry's listed as a combatant in the next match. Aside from that, there's no information about him in the system."

Kat sighed and squeezed the bridge of her nose with her fingers.

"Okay, Slaäm, tell me how I can find this Detention Facility. Let's start there."

"Riiiiight," he said slowly. "You don't know about it because it's not in any of the tourist literature, of course.

"Tell me, Kat," he said, straightening up at his desk, "how much do you know about how the Space Elevator works?"

"Um, well, the basics, I guess. You know – long wire, space station at the top, ground station on the planet, that sort of stuff."

Slaäm exhaled a long breath and said, "I'm going to make a fresh pot of coffee. We're going to need it. I'll make this as brief and as basic as I can, but you better settle in and get comfy."

*　　　　　*　　　　　*

"MUCH LIKE ON EARTH, where we've been studying this since the early 1900's, geostationary orbit here can be achieved at approximately 38,000 kilometers above the ground. That's important, because above that height, the cable itself and any structures attached to it exert an *upward* pull on the wire.

"Think of it as though you were swinging a weight on a length of rope in a complete vertical circle. When the weight is at the top of the circle, it pulls upwards, thanks to centrifugal force. And the heavier the weight, the stronger the pull. That's how the Space Elevator works. It's swinging in a circle around the planet with tremendous centrifugal force, but moving in sync with the planet so its position relative to the ground never changes.

"They put the station in orbit at only 60,000 kilometers, but even at that low altitude, its huge mass provides enough upwards pull to support the weight of the line and any payloads it might carry, and then some.

"But it needs to be anchored to the ground, of course, and as it turns out, there's no land anywhere near this planet's Equator that offers any accessible bedrock to anchor down the station. Most of it is volcanic deposits. And ocean-based platforms aren't possible because the oceans here have powerful and erratic currents.

"So they needed to mitigate the upwards pull the cable would exert on the ground-based anchor. And the solution they came up with is quite elegant.

"Because the station provides such abundant *upwards* force, they were able to tether a second, smaller facility below it at about 28,000 kilometers altitude. Because that's 10,000 kilometers below the point of geostationary orbit, that facility pulls *downwards*, and serves as a counterweight to the space station's pull, lessening the demand on the planetside anchor and providing additional stability to the wire.

"It's almost as though the entire Elevator is suspended in midair, with the smaller facility pulling downwards, and the space station pulling upwards, with just an anchor on the ground to keep it from drifting away.

"The smaller structure doesn't exert as much downward pull as the space station is exerting from above, but we don't want it to – the station still needs to provide enough additional upwards pull to support the wire and whatever else is on the cable below geostationary orbit.

"So, in the most basic terms," said Kat, draining her cup of java, "they put a prison in orbit beneath the space station, and the two facilities act as counterweights to each other. The prison benefits from its escape-proof surroundings while reducing the tension on the planetside anchor holding everything in place."

"And because it's at only 28,000 kilometers, the facility still has about 97% gravity onsite," said Slaäm.

"But you still need to access the space station to leave orbit," added Kat.

"Yes, that was the deal. The space station needs to control all transit. The prison doesn't care about that, though – they don't actually *want* anyone to be able to leave. That's sort of the whole point of a jail, don't you know."

"And I've got to get Jerry out of there in the next five days before he's murdered in this 'death match'. And unless I'm severely misjudging them, the people holding him are probably the same people who are moving the Agresso off-planet, so they're not likely to be anxious to help me."

"That's putting it mildly, I would think, Kat. And while I understand you wanting to spring Jerry, you do understand the concept of a maximum-security prison, don't you? They tend to frown on unscheduled departures."

"Yeah, I get that. How much do you know about the Detention Center?"

"Quite a bit, actually – they have their own Engineering crew, but they're still part of the whole Elevator system, so we have access to their schematics. And no, Kat, I can't sneak you in there as part of an Engineering maintenance team. They are extremely touchy about who they let onsite. We could never swing access for you, at least not in the time frame you need."

"Well, what can you tell me about their physical layout? Maybe there's something I can use there."

"Hm. I'm not so sure.

"The Detention Center is a gigantic torus – a huge donut, if you will – surrounding the cable. It's held in place by a strong magnetic field powered by an onsite fusion reactor.

"The regular Elevators pass right through without even slowing down. There's a special Elevator used purely for prison trips. The Elevator docking platform is on the exact opposite side of the torus from the Interrogation rooms and the prisoner confinement areas.

"Anyone trying to leave the prison and get to the Elevator would have to pass through more than a dozen barred gates, all of which use old-fashioned metal locks with keyholes. That's by design. No hacker can tap into the system and open the gates remotely. They each have to be opened by hand, by a different guard, using different keys. There is no Master key.

"Even if you could get to the Elevator landing area, you would need a craft scheduled to stop and accept passengers, and departure is possible only when a guard remotely monitoring the Elevator enters an "OK" code, at which point, yes, you guessed it, another guard onsite has to manually pull a release lever to allow the craft to exit.

"There *is* a maintenance bay near the center of the torus, where robotic maintenance craft enter and exit the facility, but there's no oxygen in the bay. It's pressurized, but with argon, an inert, non-toxic gas. They use argon because it's an extremely stable element with non-reactive properties. You can't breathe it, though. If you tried, you'd die."

"Why pressurize the maintenance bay at all?"

"For the same reason the maintenance bots are pressurized – there's some very sensitive equipment in place that might be damaged in an unpressurized environment. Pressurizing the surroundings allows us to control several environmental factors, such as temperature."

"Tell me about these maintenance bots. What do they do?"

"Well, the diamond nanothread cable needs regular maintenance, so that micrometeors or other space debris that impact it don't end up creating a cascade failure that will bring down the whole cable. The hafnium boride ceramic coating protects it pretty well, but there's still the possibility of minor damage getting through.

"Hence these maintenance bots. There's a few hundred of them patrolling the wire at all times, electronically scanning for damage and either repairing anything they find or reporting it so that a full maintenance team can come restore the section. There's a lot of redundant capability built into the cable, so, as long as minor damage is constantly repaired, there's no danger of a catastrophic failure.

"Now, like I mentioned, the maintenance bots are pressurized, to protect sensitive instruments and various systems inside the craft, but, again, with argon. There's no life support. It's possible to fit a human body into the craft – just barely – but without oxygen they're no good for transit, unless you're wearing a spacesuit."

"But why would they even have room for a human passenger, if they're robotic maintenance craft?"

"It's an extra layer of utility, in case a tech needs to visually inspect some damage in person or manually handle a repair procedure, and no larger craft are readily available. A lot depends on keeping this cable intact, and they didn't cut corners in their maintenance plans."

"Where do they keep the EV suits in the facility?"

"They don't. And not by accident. There are no EV suits or any other gear that would allow you to exit the facility. There's not even any emergency oxygen supplies. If there's an emergency or other catastrophic event that vents the air onsite, everyone there dies. Period."

"You're not being very encouraging, Slaäm."

"It's a *prison,* Kat. What were you expecting – a McDonald's drivethru?"

They sat there for a moment, just looking at each other, then Kat straightened up and said, "Well, I'll figure something out, Slaäm. What I need from you now is a speedy passage up to the station proper. What's the fastest trip this Elevator offers?"

"Probably not fast enough, Kat. There's a Rapid Express you could catch tomorrow, and that's almost a two-day trip. And then you'd still have to make your way back down to the prison on a separate craft."

Kat looked exasperated.

"No, there's got to be a faster way."

"Well," said Slaäm quietly, "there *is* something else, but it's not exactly comfortable."

"Screw comfort – spill it. What's the deal?"

"There's an equipment-only capsule that transports Engineering supplies on an accelerated trajectory, but there's no food, no bathroom facilities, and minimal life support. In fact, we only included basic life support in the design at the last minute, in case we ever needed to send technicians up in an emergency.

"You'd be traveling at high G's for much of the trip, both accelerating and decelerating, but it's not enough to kill you. You won't like it, though."

"How long?"

"We can make that trip in ten hours. We don't have one scheduled but I can handle that. We need to get you out of that peasant clothing and into a jumpsuit, and then hunt you down some rations and… comfort garments…. I can sneak you onboard without running any paperwork. You might have some trouble at the top when you try to exit, but I have a feeling that's the least of your worries."

"Yeah, that won't be a problem. How soon can I leave?"

"Um, one hour?"

"Let's go find those diapers."

NOT ONE OF Slaäm's technicians even raised an eyebrow when he slipped Kat onto the Elevator. The Chief could do no wrong, in their opinion.

"Since you're the only cargo, we might even be able to beat our previous speed record, Kat," he said cheerfully as he helped her strap in to the pressure seat.

"Hey, ten hours will do just fine, Slaäm. I'm not really interested in arriving in pancake shape."

He chuckled and said, "Don't worry. I'll personally monitor your status for the entire trip – I should have gotten some of those diapers for myself. Until you're safely on the station I'm not leaving the Control Room."

Kat reached up and gave him a kiss on the cheek.

"Thanks, Slaäm. I owe you a big one."

"Go get Jerry. You can thank me when we're all back together sharing a keg of beer."

Turning around quickly, he bolted the hatch shut from the outside, then waved at his techs. The Elevator lurched into motion, and Kat felt herself being pressed back into her chair.

The G forces were only slightly higher than what Kat had experienced on the trip down, but there was no free-fall respite. The chamber went directly from constant acceleration mode to immediate deceleration.

The chair Kat was strapped into was on a swiveling mount that drunkenly swung round when the momentum switched. Kat felt like she was on an amusement park ride, but the kind they have in Hell, where the ride never ends and you can't get off.

To kill time, she watched some amusing cat videos on Universe-Tube, and then did a search to find out what a "McDonald's drive through" is.

To her great relief, she didn't need to change her comfort wear during the trip, but didn't really feel like eating, either. Turns out a sandwich isn't all that appealing when it weighs five pounds.

When the craft finally arrived at the station Kat unbuckled the seat harness and collapsed onto the floor. After being pressed down for ten hours, she felt like she was floating, but her muscles still screamed at her.

She opened the little tin she got from Mathilde and ate a tiny chunk of the Agresso, then sighed as she felt the strength of ten men coursing through her body. She had a new appreciation for those Popeye cartoons Jerry forced her to watch.

Moving over to the hatch, she spun the locking wheel and pushed it open, stepping out onto the landing platform where a surprised tech goggled at her.

"Security," said Kat. "Get me a Security person ASAP."

The tech nodded wordlessly and quickly tapped out a code on the tablet he carried. Within sixty seconds two burly guards burst into the staging area and spotted Kat, then warily approached her.

"I need to speak with the Head of Security immediately," she said. "And the General Manager of the station, too, if he or she is around."

"And why should we bother these people just because you want to see them?" asked one of the guards.

"Because they'll want to see me. Tell them Juanita Falcòn sent me."

They ushered Kat into a shuttle and whizzed through the concourse at breakneck speed, honking the horn and waving pedestrians out of the way. She was shown into a small office and within minutes two executive-looking types came in through another door.

"Carla DeMarco, Station Manager," said an attractive woman in her late fifties, shaking Kat's hand with a firm grip. "And this is Neil Herie, GSC Chief of Security and Station Liaison," indicating the solid, heavyset man to her left.

The GSC man didn't bother extending his hand but just nodded at Kat and said curtly, "You mentioned Agent Falcòn sent you. When was the last time you spoke with her?"

"I might have misled your men to save time," said Kat. "Agent Falcòn is dead, killed by the smugglers you're after, but I have this —" and she pulled out the watch and laid it on the desk — "and I have the data that's encoded on it."

"We already knew Juanita is dead," said Ms. DeMarco. "One of our other agents reported it to us several days ago. We thought the entire operation had been ruined. I can't say it's not a shock to see the watch. We thought it was gone forever, along with any chance of discovering the identity of the people behind all this. But now you say you've managed to extract the data, as well? How did you manage that?"

"That's not really important," said Kat. "What *is* important is that my partner has been captured by the thugs who killed Agent Falcòn, and they're holding him in the Detention Center. They've also scheduled him for a so-called 'death match' in five days' time. More like three days, now. I need you to have him released without delay, and delivered live and kicking to the station."

"That won't be possible," said Herie. "We don't have any power over the Detention Facility. It's under the auspices of the planetary government, and out of our reach. We can petition the Governing Council and send them a strongly-worded message, but that's the extent of our influence."

"I suspected as much," said Kat. "It's no wonder they've been able to run a smuggling operation under your noses for the last fifteen years – you're so wound up in bureaucracy and protocol you're like helpless children trying to negotiate with your kindergarten teacher for more recess time."

"Now hold on just one moment," said the GSC man, starting to get a little red under his collar. "You've got no call to barge in here and start talking like that to us."

"HEY!" Kat shouted, slamming her palm down on the table. "I've got *every* right when the brutal thugs you've been playing patty-cake with for a decade and a half have strangled me, shot arrows at me, tried to feed me to carnivorous monsters, and kidnapped my partner, all because you're too incompetent to snuff out a simple smuggling ring!

"Now you listen to me," she continued, speaking rapidly enough that neither of them could interrupt her, "I've uploaded into your computer just a smidgin of the data your technical geniuses couldn't even detect, and if you want the rest of it, you'll help me get my partner out of that murder hole. Don't worry, you don't need to do anything that will violate your precious 'diplomatic protocols' – all I want is for you to turn a blind eye to my presence on this station, and arrange an Elevator that will cart me down to the prison.

"I'll be sure you have all the clearances from them in your system, but I've got no time to dick with your procedural delays. Make it happen, Sir and Madam, and I'll provide you with enough evidence to lock up the entire Governing Council until the stars burn out."

She finished talking and stood there panting, then said:

"So tell me – do we have a deal?"

Herie opened his mouth to speak, but DeMarco cut him off with a sharp motion of her hand.

"We do indeed, my dear," she said, smiling at Kat and extending her hand again. "You just tell us what you need and you shall have it."

HERIE WALKED KAT OUT to the concourse and said brusquely, "When do you want to leave for the detention facility?"

"I need to get a couple of items delivered first. Let's do it in…." She made a quick calculation in her head. "In 60 hours. That should give me enough time to get my ducks in a row and travel down to the prison. How fast can we make that trip?"

"We have a turbo that can do it in four hours. That fast enough for you?"

Kat shuddered at the thought of more high-G abuse, but put it out of her mind and said, "Perfect. I'll see you at the prison transport bay in 60 hours."

Kat scurried over to a small café. After using their bathroom to change out of her diaper, she grabbed a coffee and sat down at a table in the back.

"Call Brian," she told her glasses. Immediately she heard a ringtone in her ear, and after three pulses a cheerful voice said, "As I live and breathe! Kat! What a nice surprise! Are you calling to tell me you're onplanet and want to buy me a beer, or is there another, less-delightful reason for your call?"

Kat laughed pleasantly and said, "Sorry to disappoint you, Bri, but this is more business than pleasure. I'll be sure to remember you for brewskies the next time I'm on Gamma Cephei, though. Right now I need your help and it's kind of an urgent matter."

"Say no more, Kat. Tell me what you need and it shall be done."

"Awesome. Tell me, Brian, are you still working with those experimental EVA suits? If you are, then here's what I need...."

Kat left the café feeling happy, but still needed to get her supplies in hand. Across the concourse from her she spotted a little kiosk with a familiar cartoon logo of a delivery man leaning out the window of a little cartoon spaceship.

Walking up to the counter, she said to the clerk, "How fast can you make a delivery here from Gamma Cephei?"

The clerk tapped away on a tablet and said, "72 hours."

"Not fast enough," said Kat.

"Um, well, we do have an expedited service, but it's significantly more expensive. You might—"

Kat cut him off.

"How fast is that one?"

"Um... let's see... 58 hours."

"Nope," said Kat. "Try again."

"Ma'am," said the attendant, "you *do* realise how far away Gamma Cephei is, don't you?"

"Yes, and I also realise that money can work miracles. Now listen carefully: I don't care what it costs, money is of absolutely no concern to me. Now tap away at that pad of yours some more and tell me that you can bring me a package from Gamma Cephei in 48 hours."

The clerk gulped and went to work again on his tablet, then said, "We can do it, but you'll have to pay in advance, and the number is pretty high."

Kat tapped her teeth together and did something with her eyes and then said, "Will that cover it?"

Confused, the clerk looked back down at his display, then said, "YES MA'AM!"

"Good," said Kat. "I just uploaded all the pickup information. The package is ready now. I'll be back here in exactly 48 hours to pick it up. If it's not here waiting for me I hope you can breathe vacuum."

And turning on her heel, she strode away, hopped into an idle shuttle, and whizzed off in search of a quiet hotel.

22

THIS TIME, when the pinprick of light returned, it grew much more quickly, and suddenly Jerry could see again. He flicked his eyes from side to side, scanning the room he was laying in.

"Oh good, you've come round. Take a deep breath, and in a moment your senses will clear."

The doctor looking down at Jerry seemed kindly enough, but Jerry could sense the man was no friend.

"Where am I," Jerry whispered through a throat that felt dry and sore.

"You're in the medical facility located in the Planetary Detention Center. You've been here for six days now. You took a nasty blow to the head, and we've had to wait for the bleeding around your brain to stop and the swelling to subside before we could risk waking you up."

"Detention Center? Why am I in a Detention Center?"

"That's not for me to explain, unfortunately. My job is just to fix you fellows up, not ask why you're here. But one of the guards is on his way over right now. I'm sure he can explain everything to you."

Almost on cue, a burly man wearing a snug jumpsuit entered the room and strode directly over to Jerry's bedside, where he stood looking down at him.

"Decided to return to the land of the living, have we?" said the man, a malicious grin twisting his face. "Just in time, too. I was told to push you out an airlock if you still couldn't talk."

"What is it you want from me?" croaked Jerry.

"We want you to tell us how to get the information off that watch of yours, and who you got it from.

"After that, we're done. You help us out and we'll cut you loose."

"And straight into an open airlock," rasped Jerry.

"That all depends on what you tell us, and how long you make us wait."

Looking up at the doctor, the man said, "Yank those tubes off him and get him ready to move. We're taking him to Interrogation."

"I'm not sure tha—"

"No. We did it your way. Now we do it my way. Put him on a gurney if you have to, but get him to Interrogation right now, one way or another."

"See you soon, asshole," the man said, looking back down at Jerry, and then turned and left the room.

They dragged Jerry to a small windowless room and shackled his hands to a ring mounted in the center of a metal table bolted to the floor, then sat him down on a metal chair also bolted in place.

The big man he'd seen in the medical bay came in and placed a long leather billy club down on the table, and, beside it, Jerry's Patek Philippe watch.

"Tell us how to get the information off that watch," he said.

"I can't," said Jerry. "There's no information on that watch."

The man picked up the leather sap and brought it down hard on Jerry's hands. Shafts of pain shot through his fingers.

"That was just a tap. I got more where that came from. And don't worry – I won't be hitting you in the head. I'm not interested in waiting another week while you recover in sick bay. But you've got lots of other real estate here for me to work on, and when I've pounded the shit out of you, I can start cutting parts off. I'll probably start with your nuts.

"Now let's try that again: tell us how to read that watch."

"Okay…" said Jerry, "let's see, how should I begin? Well, when Mickey's little hand is on the two, and his big hand is on the twel—"

The sap came down again on his fingers, and this time Jerry saw stars, the pain was so intense.

"I can see we're going to be at this a while," said the man grimly. "But I'm an optimist. I believe in people. I think you're a smart guy, and that you want to help me out, and you don't want any more nasty raps on those knuckles, so I'll ask you just one, last, friggin' time, dipshit. How do we get the information from that watch?"

"How do you get down from an elephant?" Jerry asked, directing a beady stare at the man.

"Huh?"

"You don't," said Jerry flatly, answering his own question. "You get down from a duck."

"What in hell are you talking about?"

"I'm trying to tell you there's no information on that watch. It's just a watch."

"You expect me to believe you have that thing with you just to tell the time?"

"Well, that, and there's the fashion aspect, too – I've always wondered why women get to wear all the—"

The sap came down again on the fingers, and Jerry gasped in shock as the pain lanced up through his arms.

"You're a piece of work, buddy," said the man, then turned to his side away from Jerry and, pressing his finger against his earbud, said quietly, "Has that guy arrived yet?... Good. Get him over to Interrogation 3. Right away."

A minute later the door behind Jerry opened and a small, bespectacled man in his late seventies or early eighties, wearing a herringbone suit and a bow tie, entered the room.

"I want you to tell me about that," said the big man, pointing at Jerry's watch.

The little man's eyes lit up when he saw the timepiece. He scurried over to the other side of the table and sat down, then pulled the watch over.

"Ohh, this is nice…" he cooed, picking up the watch and cradling it in his palm as though it were a baby bird.

"Patek Philippe, early 1900's, Breguet balance spring, micrometer regulator, 23 jewels, triple signed with rare barrel lugs and—

"Wait." The man stopped talking and frowned slightly. "This watch has been opened by someone."

The big man smiled smugly. "Now we're getting somewhere," he said with satisfaction.

The little man put a small tool kit on the table and extracted a couple of delicate instruments. Turning the watch over, he deftly worked away at it for a moment, then carefully eased the case open and laid the watch face-down on the table, then gently extracted the clockwork movement.

He looked up in disgust.

"Is this some kind of joke?" he said to the big man.

"What are you talking about?"

"This is no Swiss watch. It's a fake."

Fake? thought Jerry, puzzled.

"Look at this movement. There's a name marked there."

"What does it say?" asked the big man, curious. Both he and Jerry were craning their necks to get a closer look at the watch.

"It says 'TIMEX'," said the little man in an offended tone.

"You're wasting my time. This is nothing but a cheap, fake knock-off watch from the mid-twentieth-century. There's nothing special about it at all. I wouldn't give you even one credit for it."

And throwing his tools back into the case, he stood up and left the room.

The big man and Jerry looked at each other in silence.

"Told ya," said Jerry.

Jerry expected the sap to come down again on his fingers, but instead the big man just turned away and walked over to the corner.

Jerry's thoughts were awhirl. *So that miserly grandfather of mine didn't honour his debt after all. The old cheapskate probably took the real watch to his grave with him, just out of pure spite. And to think I went to his funeral! I should have searched the coffin. The bastard.*

Jerry heard the big man quietly talking again to his confederates through his earbud.

"No," the man murmured, "it's a ruse. There's nothing there...." He paused. There was great consternation on the other end. "An expert? You don't need that. I can handle this guy myself.... Fine. I'll stick him in a cell and we'll let your guy take a whack at him. But don't expect to get anything useful. There's something wrong with this asshole. He's not taking this seriously at all. I think maybe we might have hit him in the head one too many times…. Fine. Like I said, go ahead and bring your guy in – when it comes right down to it, all we really need is the name of who he got it from. That shouldn't be too hard to extract."

The big man walked quickly over to Jerry and smiled down at him.

"I'm sorry, but our time together has come to an end," he said, grinning. "But I have a feeling you'll just love my replacement."

He turned and walked out of the room, and as the door swung shut, Jerry heard him say to someone outside, "Stick him in a cell somewhere out of sight. We got an *'expert'* coming to talk to this jerkoff."

23

JERRY WAS CURLED UP shivering on the floor of a windowless cell, stripped down to a pair of boxer shorts, without even a bench to lay on, when a guard opened the door and yanked him to his feet.

"Let's go, jerkoff. Time to start singing."

The guard pushed/pulled him along the corridor and threw him back into the interrogation room, shoved him down into the metal chair and shackled his hands once again to the metal table. Then he left the room to take up his post outside the door guarding the exit.

A moment later three people filed into the room. One was the guard who had interrogated Jerry the previous day, another was a nasty-looking individual dressed in a dark suit over a black polo shirt.

They both leaned against the wall near the door, and while the guard stood there glaring at him, the second man ignored him and instead studiously examined his own fingernails as though he hoped to find a set of winning lottery numbers inscribed on them.

The third person was a short, heavy-set woman with mousy blonde hair pulled back in a severe bun tight against her head.

"This should be quite an educational experience for us," said the first guard smugly, as Jerry looked curiously at the little group. "Apparently the guy coming to, ah, *question* you, is pretty effective at his trade. I can't speak for my coworkers here, but I'm sure looking forward to picking up a few pointers. My only regret will be that I wasn't able to use any of them on you."

"When is your guy getting here?" asked fingernail man.

"Apparently he's already onsite. Should be showing up in a few minutes, as soon as they can finish scanning him."

"Why are they scanning him?" asked the woman.

The first guard gave her a patronizing look.

"Because it don't matter who you are or where you're coming from, everyone gets scanned, head to toe, inside and out. Nothing and no one gets onsite without clearing the system."

The three waited in silence, tapping their feet – or staring at their fingernails, as the case may be – when the woman said, "So this dickhead is one of the prelims before tonight's Main Event?"

The first guard nodded.

"Yup, but the line totally sucks. Something like minus 6,000 for Mad Dog McCoy."

The other two laughed loudly and the woman said, "Well, hell, doesn't seem to be much confidence in this boy's survival skills, now does there?"

"The big money is on how many seconds he'll last," said fingernail man. "It's a given that it'll be a one-round fight, but he might make it past sixty seconds before McCoy removes his head from his shoulders."

"I got my money on forty seconds," said the first guard. "The line's not too bad on that. I might be able to double my money, at least.

"What I'm really looking forward to, though, is shoving his worthless carcass out the airlock afterwards. I asked if I can do it personally. For once I'll enjoy seeing one of these dickheads sucked into space. Won't give me the willies like it usually does, I can promise you that. This piece of shit might cure my jitters once and for all."

"You should work planetside if space bothers you like that," said the woman.

"Are you kidding? Slog around in that mudhole with those hopped-up cavemen? I'll take space over that any day, vacuum be damned."

Silence descended once again on the little group, until fingernail man said, "Shit. What's the holdup?"

The first guard put his finger to his earbud then said, "He's coming now."

A second later the door opened and in walked a tall brunette woman with the largest bust Jerry had ever seen. Even the suit jacket she wore couldn't conceal its prodigious size. She was wearing a dark blue business suit with stiletto heels.

The first guard gaped in consternation.

"*You're* the interrogation expert?" he said.

"Do you have a problem with that?" asked the woman evenly, staring into the guard's eyes without blinking.

"No, ah, it's just that I thought—"

"Thought *what?* That only a micro-dicked musclebound moron like you with more fat around his belly than brains in his head could make this pathetic little shit spill his guts?"

The guard stuttered something unintelligible in response. Jerry laughed and grinned at him.

"HEY!" the woman yelled at Jerry, spinning around and viciously smashing him in the mouth with her open hand, splitting open his upper lip and knocking his head backward. "Did I *tell* you you could laugh, shit for brains? NO, I sure as living FUCK did NOT tell you you could laugh. You don't even *breathe* without my permission, you worthless piece of dirt! One more sound out of you that's not a direct response to one of my questions and I'll pull your tongue right out of your empty head and nail it to your forehead.

"IS THAT CLEAR?"

Jerry just stared at the woman's eyes and nodded, silently.

"Good," said the woman firmly.

"You have my permission to keep breathing. For now."

The other guards stared openmouthed and dumbfounded at the woman. Fingernail man seemed to have forgotten all about his cuticle issues and the female guard stood wide-eyed and motionless.

The tall woman leaned back and rested against the table. She bent over and unstrapped one of her shoes and kicked it away, where it skittered across the floor and came to rest against the wall by the door, then brought her other foot up onto her knee and worked away at the buckle on the strap.

"Molten lava," she muttered. The other guards looked at each other quizzically. "That's what it feels like, like I'm standing in molten lava when I wear these things. What we won't do for fashion."

The other woman nodded sympathetically, even though it was an open question whether she'd ever done anything in her life for fashion.

The tall woman burst back to life as she tugged the second shoe free then looked up and hollered, "Great jumping Jehoshaphat, who the fuck do you have to kill around here to get a freaking cup of coffee?"

Storming over to the door, she pounded heavily on it and screamed, "Hey out there!"

The door swung open a couple of feet and the guard outside said, "Yes? Is there a problem?"

"You bet your fucking life there's a problem! I *told* them when I landed that I wanted a fucking cup of coffee! I've been here a half hour now and I STILL don't have a coffee!"

"Um, no one mentioned anything to me," the guard said tentatively. "Um, would you like me to get you a coffee?"

"No shit, Sherlock! That's some stellar deductive reasoning you've got there. I guess that's why you're not stuck away in some shithole post in the middle of nowhere watching your life slip away in front of your eyes – oh, sorry, my mistake."

Before the guard outside the door could respond, she said quietly, "Now go get me my fucking coffee." And she pulled the door shut in his face, the latch clanking heavily into place.

"Now, where were we…. Oh yes—"

Whereupon, with startling speed that rendered her movement little more than a blur, she swung out the hand that still clutched her shoe, and buried the sharpened stiletto heel three inches deep into the first guard's throat.

Before the gurgling man had hit the ground, fingernail man was already standing up and reaching into his jacket. His hand, now clasping a silver blade, had barely emerged when she delivered an upper cut to his jaw, sending him spinning around and stumbling up against the metal table.

He planted both hands on the table to break his fall, and as he did so the woman, leaping up behind him, drove her heel into the back of his knee, buckling his leg. Then she grabbed his head and slammed it against the edge of the metal table to the sound of orbital bones shattering.

Leaving him to sink to the floor, she turned and faced the goggle-eyed woman who was backing up to the far wall and edging towards the door.

"Uh-uh, sweetheart, there's no exit for you there.

"Here," she said, and in one lightning movement, she leapt at the terrified woman, spinning her around while locking her forearm around her throat. She yanked upwards viciously, producing a distinctive snapping sound. The smaller woman jerked convulsively and then went limp. The tall woman released her and let her drop to the ground, where she lay motionless, crumpled in a heap.

"*There's* your fucking exit."

The whole operation took less than fifteen seconds from start to finish, and she didn't even look out of breath.

"Nice work, Kat," said Jerry through a mouthful of blood and swollen lips. "But did you have to hit me so hard?"

"Hey Jer, when you're playing the part you're playing the part, you know what I mean? I was in the moment."

She moved over to him and kissed him deeply, almost weeping in relief to see him again. Then, straightening up, she moved back over to stand near the door, and took a couple of deep breaths to compose herself.

The minutes ticked by like hours, and Kat nervously shuffled back and forth like a tiger in a cage. Finally, a rattling sound came from the door as someone outside fiddled with the handle. Slowly, the door opened a crack, and then the toe

of a boot was wedged into the door from the outside, pulling it open slowly. The guard came into view, balancing four coffee cups in his hands as he awkwardly tried to negotiate opening the door with his foot.

"Here you go," he said cheerfully. "Four black coffees. I thought the rest of you might like some as well, so I—"

Kat grabbed a handful of the startled man's shirt and pulled him into the room. Smashing the cups upwards, she drenched his face in boiling hot coffee. He staggered backwards, screaming in pain and clawing at his face. Kat grabbed his head by the hair and started viciously bashing his face down onto her knee over and over again while screaming, "WHAT" *(smack)* "THE" *(smack)* "FUCK" *(smack)* "IS" *(smack)* "THIS???" *(smack smack smack)*.

She let go of his hair and he crumpled to the ground.

"I wanted cream and sugar in mine," she said quietly.

24

"**KAT!" CALLED JERRY,** as she caught her breath. "The door!"

"Oops!" Kat threw herself at the door as it slowly swung inwards. Just before it met the latch she stopped it, then leaned down and grabbed her discarded shoe and wedged the toe discreetly into the crack between the door and the jamb.

"He's probably got keys that will open it, but you can't be too careful.

"I guess I got a little carried away again," she said sheepishly.

"You think?" said Jerry, eyeing the pulp that was once the man's face.

Kat knelt down beside the disfigured guard and pulled the ring of keys off his belt, then moved over to the table and fumbled with them until she found the one that opened Jerry's shackles.

While he rubbed feeling back into his sore wrists, Kat reached into the breast pocket of her business suit and extracted an ugly pair of horn-rimmed glasses with thick coke-bottle lenses. She smashed them repeatedly onto the metal surface, until the frames shattered and the table was covered in glass fragments.

"Kat! What in the world—"

"Don't worry, Jerry, it would take a lot more punishment than I can give them to damage Slimlines. The frames are woven carbon nanotubes, and the smartglass is virtually indestructible."

"But then, what's all that debris on the table?"

"Hm? Oh, that's the stealth coating I had to wrap them in to get them past the security scan. Copper fiber mesh covered with wax and a brown lacquer, and metallic glass lenses over the smartglass. They scanned as nothing more than a pair of extremely ugly, normal eyeglasses."

Kat looked smug, and smiled at Jerry.

"And now, my dear, are you ready to get out of this place?"

Kat tapped her teeth together then blinked once to activate the preprogrammed sequence of commands she'd entered into her Slimlines, and five seconds later the entire prison facility went black as pitch. Even the emergency light strips along the floor stayed dark.

"Kat! I'm blind as a bat!"

"Take my hand, Jer, I can see fine. Let's go."

She pulled him outside into the corridor, then fumbled with the keys for a moment, found the one that fit in the door lock, and pushed it in then broke it off in the lock.

"Thank God for old fashioned mechanical locks," she said. "Nothing like Old School."

Leading Jerry by the hand, she ran down the corridor, found a stairwell access door and unlocked it with one of the keys on the ring. They jumped inside and ran up three flights, then stopped at a heavy pressure door.

"Where are we?" asked Jerry, completely disoriented and out of breath. "And how can you run so fast?"

"Oh, I forgot to tell you – I'm using Agresso. It's awesome stuff. Too bad my supply is used up. You'd love it."

Before he could respond, the lights in the stairwell came back on in harsh illumination.

"Did you do that?" he asked.

"Yup. But just this stairwell. They're still stumbling around in the dark back there. They don't get back their lights or power or even life support until I let them. And any electronic locks are frozen shut, too. Except for the prisoner areas. All those doors I unlocked. They should have their hands full for the foreseeable future, I should think."

"Good Lord, Kat. You don't take half measures."

"Save your praise until after you hear my escape plan, Jer. You might have something different to say then."

"But first—" And Kat started to pull off her clothes, discarding her garments until she had stripped down to her panties.

"So I'm hoping," said Jerry, "that this is one of those scenarios where they say, 'Since we're about to die, we might as well do it one last time'—"

Kat grinned at him evilly. "Not this time, Jerry. Although I have to admire your devotion to your priorities."

Picking up her bra, she proceeded to break it apart at the center, separating the cups and handing one to Jerry.

"This is a breathing apparatus. I made it myself. The cup is lined with super-compressed capsules of pure oxygen. A friend of mine developed them for use with emergency EVA suits. They're designed to burst open in sequence, very gradually, providing the user with a constant supply of oxygen. Each capsule will provide you with approximately five minutes breathing time, if you're not hyperventilating. You just strap the cup on over your face like a regular mask."

"I was wondering about the insanely padded bra. I figured it was just part of the disguise, like the brown hair."

"Nope. Function before fashion, Jer. Same with the shoes – two deadly weapons that they let walk right in through all their highfalutin security."

"Why do we need these, Kat? Are we going into space?"

"We're *already* in space, Jerry. This prison facility is almost halfway up the Space Elevator, about 28,000 kilometers above the planet's surface."

"But I still don't see why we need oxygen masks. The Elevators have life support."

"Because we're not taking an Elevator, Jerry. We're jumping out on our own."

25

"**A**LRIGHT, NOW I KNOW** your mind really has snapped, Kat. Oxygen mask or no, we can't jump into space at 28,000 kilometers above the surface and survive. We'll be frozen solid in ten seconds, or at the very least our blood vessels will burst open and we'll make a very colourful cloud of debris floating in the void."

"Well, yes, Jerry, if we jumped outside like this, but we'll actually each be enclosed in small robotic capsules that I'll program to malfunction and plunge to the ground."

"That sounds like a good plan, Kat, except of course for the part about the capsules malfunctioning and plunging to the ground. Something about that sounds kinda unappealing to me, especially if I'm going to be inside one."

Kat chuckled and leaned forward to give him a kiss on the cheek.

"O ye of little faith," she said, smiling. "These craft are designed to stay within a few meters of the cable, and programmed to avoid any passing Elevators, too. They use magnetic attraction and repulsion just like the regular Elevators, and if we disable their safety protocols, we can make them drop at freefall down to the planet's surface.

"I'm going to goose their controls a bit though, to make them add downward thrust. I don't know how high I can get our speed, but I want to keep this trip short, so I'm hoping we can get it up to maybe 20,000 kilometers per hour for the initial part of the drop. I want to reach atmosphere within about 45 minutes of leaving this facility.

"The bots will start to brake around halfway through the trip, though, at about 15,000 kilometers above the planet's surface. That way, when we start to hit atmosphere at 10,000 kilometers we won't heat up too much.

"I don't have enough data to know for sure, but our terminal velocity in atmospheric free-fall might be as low as only 2,000 kilometers an hour. That will give us ample time to decelerate to a speed where we can deploy landing chutes."

Jerry looked at Kat with absolute amazement in his eyes.

"Who are you?" he said, "And what have you done with my girlfriend?"

Kat laughed evilly and gave him another peck on the cheek.

"I spoke with Slaäm earlier and he helped me work out a lot of the numbers. He thinks I'm crazy, of course, but after all, he's just an engineer – those people are so detail-oriented, they have trouble seeing the whole picture.

"It will be a shit-show of a trip, there's no doubt about that, but once we hit atmosphere the craft will automatically adjust their rate of deceleration at specific thresholds, according to the data they receive from their altimeters and anemometers. I'll program them to gradually slow down to around 700 kilometers per hour and then, about 10,000 meters above the ground, they'll deliberately repel away from the cable to prevent accidentally damaging it, and emergency chutes will deploy. If all goes according to design, we should float down to the surface as gently as two big, metal feathers."

"Has anyone ever done this?"

"Don't be silly, Jerry. That would be suicide."

"And what about when we land? What if we hit water? The craft will probably sink like anchors. And what if more goons are waiting for us on the planet? And what about—"

"Jerry, Jerry, I don't know why you're worried about all those meaningless details.

"Just the fall alone will probably kill us."

THEY SAT IN the stairwell looking at the wall and each other, and Jerry said, "Um, Kat? Shouldn't we actually be going somewhere? What are you waiting for?"

"For the Elevator, Jer. I want to wait for the next descent to pass before we leave the facility. I'm not sure how maneuverable these bots are and the Elevator will be passing through at thousands of kilometers per hour. I'd just as soon not be in its way when it does.

"You'll know when it passes, because the whole place should shake like crazy when it crosses through the facility's magnetic field."

"I've felt that," said Jerry. "The entire structure shudders for a second. I couldn't figure out what was going on. Now I understand."

"According to my Slimlines, the next one will cross through in about seven minutes."

"Seven minutes?" said Jerry, smiling broadly. "So then we *do* have enough time to—"

Kat laughed heartily and said, "Oh baby, I'm pretty tempted, but let's save it for somewhere just a bit more romantic than a stairwell in a maximum-security prison, can't we?"

"Okay, Kat, but then you need to satisfy my other desire, and tell me how you managed to get them to bring you here as an interrogation expert. That was pretty slick."

"No, that was actually the easiest part of all, Jer. I just ferreted through the data we grabbed from that watch and identified the head honcho who's running this operation. My glasses sampled his voice from recorded public appearances he's made, then I called these crooks and impersonated him.

"The space station helped out, too, since all communications pass through their system. I fixed it so that any calls to this guy from the prison facility would be rerouted to my glasses.

"And then, because I don't trust those station personnel any farther than I can throw them, I also engineered a 'system malfunction' that disabled the regular comms channels to the Detention Center. That kept anyone from alerting them if word got out about my plans. Easy-peasy, lemon squeezie."

Jerry laughed and they high-fived, just as the facility shook with a tremendous shudder.

"Showtime, Kat."

"Okay, Jer. Now, once we open this door, we won't be able to communicate anymore. This is an emergency airlock for any maintenance techs who can't reach the main exit on the far side of the maintenance bay.

"But the airlock is big enough for only one person at a time to pass through. I think if we squeeze together as close as we can, we can probably both fit inside it. After the second door opens, there's a ten-minute delay before either door will work again. That's to prevent a stream of escapees from charging through, but it also prevents compromising the maintenance bay's atmospheric integrity.

"When we exit the airlock we'll be in a utility room where techs can leave various tools and other equipment they aren't allowed to bring into the Detention Center. There's no breathable air inside, but there should still be some simple insulated cloth jumpsuits and non-EV gear there. Even in an emergency, EV suits are absolutely *verboten* in this entire facility. We'll each put on a jumpsuit and then you just follow me. I'll put you in a bot and send it on its way."

"Is there an internal control unit in the bot?"

"No. I set up full wireless access for my Slimlines, of course, so I can control mine. But in yours you'd have to have a tablet and jack-in with a special proprietary cable. That's by design, as well. I'll program the bot for you, but once you're inside you're just a passenger."

"So if it malfunctions in any unexpected way I'm completely helpless to do anything?"

Kat just nodded.

"I dunno, Kat. I'm starting to have second thoughts about this plan."

"It's your choice Jerry. You can get in the bot, or you can go back downstairs and try to reason with the prison goons. There's no Door Number 3."

"Open the airlock, Kat. You've convinced me."

26

KAT AND JERRY strapped on their masks, and Kat did something with her jaw and the red lights on the pressure door all turned green. She stood behind Jerry and wrapped her arms tightly around his stomach, then pushed him into the tiny space in front of them. She felt the door behind her sliding shut and scraping roughly against her butt. There was a loud *whooshing* sound all around them, and then they both tumbled forward as the door in front of Jerry rapidly slid open.

They stumbled out of the airlock into the utility room. Kat's eyes widened in panic as she saw only one tattered jumpsuit hanging from a peg. All the other pegs were empty. There was no other protective clothing in the room.

Twigging immediately to the problem, Jerry grabbed the jumpsuit and shoved it into Kat's hands. She shook her head, but Jerry just pointed meaningfully at her tiny underwear, then brought his fists up to his chest and thumped it heavily, like Tarzan. Kat's eyes crinkled with laughter and she nodded, then proceeded to step into the jumpsuit and zip it up.

With a rapid combination of blinks and teeth clicks, Kat released the access door and they stepped into a wide, open space, eerily lit with scattered LED fixtures bleeding out little islands of illumination. Jerry's eyes gradually adjusted to the light and he began to see more clearly where Kat was leading him.

They ran over to a line of bright orange metal capsules with little claws on extendible arms. The capsules were lined up neatly above a series of little hatches in the floor outlined with angry yellow and black dotted lines.

DO NOT STAND HERE could be read on one of the hatches that had no capsule on it.

Jerry leaned over and ran his hands over a capsule but couldn't find any latch or release mechanism. Kat tugged him back gently then clicked her teeth, and immediately a little round port cover popped up.

She helped Jerry climb in, then clicked her teeth again, and the port silently retracted and sealed.

Godspeed, baby, she whispered in her mind. Then, running over to another capsule, opened it the same way, climbed inside, and sealed the cover above her head.

Kat activated the launch procedure, and watched Jerry's capsule disappear from sight, the hatch closing up behind it. She activated her own bot and her capsule swooshed down, plunging her into the darkness of space. She caught sight of the prison facility through a little viewport as she tumbled away, and could see the access hatch snapping shut.

FOR THE FIRST quarter hour, Kat just huddled in the cramped capsule and strained against the chair restraints to see out the little viewport, but suddenly it occurred to her: several cameras are mounted all over the exterior of the craft – *duh!* She linked in to their feed with her Slimlines and was presented with a 360-degree panoramic view of her surroundings as she plunged faster and faster towards the planet's surface.

She was pleased to note that her bot was maintaining a respectable distance from the Elevator cable, but not letting her drift away. She panned through the camera feeds until she caught sight of Jerry's capsule, a little farther below her than he should be. Then she realised that he was falling just a microsecond faster than she was.

That makes no sense, she thought. *All objects fall at the same speed in a vacuum, and I set equal amounts of thrust on both bots.* The only explanation was that his craft was malfunctioning, perhaps providing greater downward thrust than she had programmed in. *I must have overestimated his increased mass – that would account for a higher rate of acceleration. Or would that result in* decreased *acceleration?...*

Her head hurt. Even with her Slimlines to help, these calculations were taxing her brain.

Well, whether the blame lay with her, or some malfunction in his machine, she didn't like that Jerry was moving farther away from her. She'd thought they'd be close together for the whole descent. She crossed her fingers and hoped that was the only way his craft was misbehaving.

Kat checked the instrument panel in front of her. She understood the altimeter but the anemometer, which measures wind speed, was useless until she hit atmosphere. There was a Doppler Shift readout to display her velocity, but its numbers meant nothing to her.

She pulled up the stats on her Slimlines, though, and was able to translate the data into numbers she could understand. They were still at least half an hour away from hitting atmosphere, and her speed was already 18,700 kilometers per hour and steadily increasing. She shuddered at the thought, then shuddered again when she contemplated the brutal

G-forces that would be required to slow her down to around 700 kph, where her chute could safely deploy. *Maybe this wasn't such a good idea after all,* she reflected morosely.

To take her mind off it, Kat called up the technical specs on the bot and scanned through the list of capabilities built into the unit.

There were clamps, and a variety of welding devices and precision tools, magnetic tethers and cutting devices, brushes, scrapers, and what appeared to be some kind of glue analog, as well as a supply of nanobot repair units.

Bots within bots. What am I *doing here?*

Tentatively, she tried operating the little extendible claw arms, but a blinking red light made her immediately cancel the operation. *Oh, that makes sense.* It was dangerous to deploy extendible parts while under thrust. The craft didn't care if it was in a vacuum – if parts were still extended when the bot hit atmosphere, they would either be ripped right off the craft or at the very least they would affect the airstream properties and send the unit into a death spin. She recoiled at the idea.

Mustn't do that again, she thought.

As the time passed during her descent, Kat kept a camera permanently focused on Jerry. He was no more than a small dot now, and the camera was zoomed to maximum magnification.

Kat busied herself running through a variety of acceleration/deceleration formulae, trying to assess which would provide the maximum time savings with tolerable associated G-forces.

She felt the craft swivel on its axis as its automatic braking procedures kicked in. Oh good, we'll be hitting atmosphere soon.

Within minutes, she looked up from her calculations as the first bright flashes of light began to streak across the viewport. Kat realised she was finally hitting the compressive force of the atmosphere. The craft started to shake a bit and she pressed herself back firmly into the chair. But it wasn't really made for high-G cushioning, and her muscles already ached. This wasn't going to be fun.

The shaking became more and more violent, and the sound of rushing wind rose from just a howl to a deafening roar.

Then, without warning, the craft's failsafe kicked in and the bot jerked as though it had just hit a wall. The straps tightened on Kat's shoulders and chest and her head was pulled violently backward, but gradually the shaking became less intense and the craft seemed much more stable.

Kat unclenched her jaw and reflexively glanced at the camera feed showing Jerry's bot. She caught her breath.

His chute had prematurely deployed, long before it should have, and worse, it was fatally tangled. She saw Jerry's bot spinning wildly and within seconds it was wrapped-up in the chute, which fully enveloped the bot like a glop of wavering meringue.

Kat knew immediately there was no recovery from that. In a few moments the bot would repel itself away from the cable and Jerry would tumble the last 10,000 meters to the ground at several times the speed of sound, probably somewhere around Mach 4. Not only would he be obliterated, but his impact crater would probably be the size of a football field.

Now that's *what I call a design flaw,* she thought.

Kat's mind raced frantically. She was helpless herself, and Jerry's capsule was too far ahead of her to do anything about, anyways.

The she realised she was wrong on both counts.

One, she wasn't helpless – she had all the assembled tools and mechanisms of her own bot to try to do something to save Jerry's, and second, Jerry was no longer as far ahead of her. The combination of his bot's obviously faulty braking procedure and the premature deployment of his chute had significantly slowed his rate of descent, at least in relation to her own.

The chute, while nowhere near effective enough to slow him down to avoid absolute obliteration, was still interfering with the aerodynamics of the craft, lowering its terminal velocity significantly. She was actually catching up fairly quickly.

Kat told her Slimlines to disable all her bot's automatic deceleration – forget fly-by-wire, she was going to have to go conventional on this trip.

Kat's mind raced through all her possible means of interfering with Jerry's craft.

She could ram into it of course, and hit it like a cue ball smacking an eight-ball, but that would do little except accelerate his descent and decelerate hers.

The little mechanical arms were useless – they were designed for precision work. Even if she did manage to grip some part of Jerry's bot with them, the first twist of his craft would probably rip them both off their mounts.

She quickly scanned the list she had read through before.

Clamps – no.

Welding tools – no.

Precision tools – no.

Magnetic tether – no. Wait. What? *Yes!* That one was a definite YES.

She called up the tether controls and scanned the options frantically. One parameter was "force".

That must mean force of attraction! At least, I hope *that's what the idiot engineer who wrote up these specs meant.* It wouldn't be the first time she'd encountered a totally illogical function coupled with misleading terminology.

Oh well, Kat, hope for the best, right? Maybe this is the one engineer in the universe who speaks the same normal English that the rest of us do. There's a first time for everything.

She checked the camera feed. Jerry's craft was getting perilously close to hers. It was less than 500 meters away now, and she was closing the gap quickly.

Kat dialed the "force" parameter to maximum and centered Jerry's craft on the tether readout. There was a set of little crosshairs on the readout, so obviously this device was meant to be deployed from a distance – at least a minimal distance, anyways.

Kat worried about the buffeting from the atmosphere, though. If the wind shear pushed the tether off course, she might not have time for a second try, if one was even possible. It wasn't immediately clear how she could retract the cable for another go at it.

She waited until the distance between their two bots was no more than about ten meters, and then pressed the button. She felt the kick beneath her feet as the tether exploded out from its barrel and watched in her glasses' display as the wide, flat saucer of the tether's end impacted with Jerry's bot and firmly adhered.

Almost immediately, her craft rammed against Jerry's and, just as she had predicted, sent it rocketing downwards as her own slowed noticeably in its descent.

Perfect.

Jerry's bot continued its rapid descent, trailing a long line behind it that disappeared out of her camera's vision into the belly of her own bot.

As the tether reached its full length, Kat was jerked upwards in her seat as Jerry's bot yanked down on the line.

But it held.

Regretting it before she did it, Kat reactivated her craft's failsafe braking procedure and was once again slammed back into her chair. Clenching her teeth through the crushing G-force, she felt blackness descending over her. She was passing out from the unbearable force, and only just managed to activate the full auto control in her Slimlines' display before the darkness swallowed her up.

**IME TO WAKE UP,** baby.”

Pause.

“C'mon, Kat, wakey-wakey.

“No more nap time for you.”

Confusion.

“Up and at 'em, kitty-kat.”

Kat's eyes flickered open.

“*Finally!* I was about to go get a bucket of water to throw on your face.”

Kat looked up groggily into Jerry's eyes. They looked back down at her with concern, but there was a good measure of relief mixed in, as well.

She raised her head slightly to look around her. She was on her back in a virtual lake of mud. Jerry was coated in mud, and it dripped from his body as he sat back on his haunches.

“Oh, God, Jerry, not more mud….”

He laughed heartily and said, “Given the choice between mud and vacuum, I think I'll take mud any day.”

“Why does my head hurt so bad, Jerry?”

“Um, gee, I dunno babe – do you think it might have something to do with explosively decelerating at 5 or 6 G's for several minutes? That's just a guess, though, I couldn't say for sure.”

“Is that blood on your face?”

"Mm-hm. And on yours, too, but I think a couple of nosebleeds is a small price to pay for…" and here Jerry's voice dropped into a deep intonation, "*going where no man has gone before!* Dum-dum-dum!"

"Dumb is right. And we didn't go anywhere new, we just jumped out of a suborbital space facility and fell to the ground. Big whupp."

"Oh yeah, I forgot. People do that every day."

Kat sat upright and rubbed her temples, then lifted a mud-caked hand to her face to wipe away some of the dried blood. She looked around her.

They were sitting in a huge marsh, about fifteen feet from an orange metal capsule that lay almost completely submerged in the muck. A long trail of cables were splayed out around it, leading to a wide, billowing white cloud that rustled in the wind.

"Is that my chute? When did it deploy? I blacked out when we were still next to the wire."

Jerry shrugged.

"I dunno. It must have deployed on cue, according to plan. To tell the truth, I was out cold as well. I woke up here, sitting in my capsule." He indicated with a flick of his thumb another orange capsule just barely visible above the mud about 50 meters away. "I climbed out and followed that anchor cable and made my way over here and dragged you out of yours."

Jerry suddenly stopped smiling and his expression became serious as he looked at her.

"You saved my life, Kat. If you hadn't hooked on to my bot, I would have died."

"Does that mean you need to call your lawyer now?"

"What are you talking about, Kat?"

"You said the day you need me to save your bacon is the day you'll need to get your will in order. I figured— *Hey!* What's the idea? Why did you fling that mud at me?"

"I can't *believe* you, Kat. Here I am, all serious and all, and the only thing on your mind is rubbing it in what I jerk I've been!"

"Well, lah-de-dah. The big man doesn't like it so much when the chickens come home to roost, now does he?

Jerry just looked at her grumpily.

"Awww, wassamatta, is the widdow man's feewings all hurt by the big bad Kat wady?"

Jerry jumped on Kat and started wrestling her into the mud, while they both giggled furiously.

Flopping back in the mud, puffing heavily, Jerry looked at her and said, "You still have a lot to learn Kat. Haven't you ever read Sun-Tzu where he says you have to give your opponent an opportunity to save face?"

"No, but I've read Confucius where he says that what's good for the goose—"

"Don't finish that thought, Kat, or there's another handful of mud coming your way!"

Giggling, Kat rolled up onto her feet and, wiping the blood and mud off her Slimlines, grabbed Jerry's hand and pulled him up out of the muck.

"C'mon, my Brave and Handsome Knight, let's walk to that ground station over there and find a warm bath and some clean clothes. I happen to have a suite reserved in a certain French hotel, and I'll bet they stock just the absolute *best* Champagne…."

OT WANTING to barge in on her guests unannounced, Kat called the hotel and asked the manager to give Mathilde a heads-up that they were on their way.

She and Jerry almost fell out of their shuttle when it pulled up to the hotel. They dragged themselves into the foyer, leaving a trail of muddy dirt clumps in their wake.

"How nice to see you again, mademoiselle," said the manager, eyeing the destruction to the previously spotless floor. "I trust you had an enjoyable visit to the planet?"

Kat trained a well-practiced fish eye on him and said, "Oh yes. Everything we hoped for. We even brought some of it back for you, as a little present." As she said this, a particularly large wedge of dried mud broke free from her jumpsuit and splattered on the marble flooring.

"You really shouldn't have," said the hotelier.

Just then, Kat heard Mathilde calling out to her from the lobby beyond the front desk. She looked closely but couldn't spot the woman among the various guests milling about.

"Kat!" called the voice again, and Kat followed the sound, coming from behind a group of well-heeled tourists clustered near the elevator.

"Kat!" cried the voice again, and one of the rich tourists broke away from her group, ran over and gave Kat a big hug.

"Oh my God!" exclaimed Kat. "Mathilde, is that you? And, and— this dapper gentleman can't be Elric?! And who is this darling little girl?"

The trio laughed heartily. Looking a bit sheepish, Elric chuckled, "Me own mother wouldn't recognise me, I daresay, Miss Kat. Look at what they've gone and given me to wear. They took me old clothes and won't give them back."

"They made me wear a *dress*," said the child, enunciating the word as though it hurt her mouth to say it.

"And I see you got your young man back," said Mathilde, looking Jerry up and down with a critical eye.

A discreet cough behind Kat caught her attention and she turned to the manager, who was standing at her left shoulder.

"Yes?"

"Ah, well, as delightful as it is to have you back on the premises, mademoiselle, the hotel does maintain a… shall we say… *dress code* within its public areas."

"Your point being?"

"Well, normally we request that our guests refrain from strolling around the reception area in just their underwear…."

Kat looked over at Jerry in mock horror and said loudly, "Jerry! *What* have you done with the rest of your clothes? Do we have to have this conversation again, young man?"

The manager gave her another of those weak smiles of his, but before he could say anything further she proclaimed, "Say no more. We're on our way up to the *Charlemagne* suite right away. We'll be indisposed until the morning. I've uploaded our measurements and clothing preferences into your computer. Do you think it's within your couturier's capabilities to furnish us with garments by the morning?"

"Absolutely, mademoiselle, we have the fi—"

He saw Kat grinning at him and he coughed, then said, "Would 7am be soon enough?"

"Only if your couturier has a death wish. I wouldn't advise anyone knocking on our door before noon. Better yet, wait until we've had breakfast. We'll call you when we want it sent up.

"In the meantime, does the hotel have any Champagne in stock? You do? Good. Send up a couple of magnums of Château Lafite to the suite right away. I want it there before the tub gets filled."

Kat heard Jerry clear his throat behind her and she said, "Sorry, I meant to say three—" *cough cough* —"I mean, *four* magnums."

She glanced over at Jerry, then added, "And two orders of *steak frites*. Burned on the outside, raw in the middle. The steaks that is, not the frites.

"And that's *cow*, I'm referring to, buddy. Not *cheval*."

"Mademoiselle is too amusing," said the hotelier, slipping away before Kat could ask for a dessert menu.

29

KAT DIDN'T REMEMBER to call Slaäm until she was halfway through her fourth glass of bubbly, so her report on their terrifying descent from the prison facility was heavily punctuated with giggling fits, all at the most inappropriate moments.

"Oh Lord," said Slaäm in horror. "Jerry's capsule malfunctioned and the chute wrapped around it?"

"Yes!" howled Kat in hysterics. "He almost died! Both of us! We both almost died!" Convulsed with laughter, she and Jerry howled away while Slaäm held the phone away from his ear, and contemplated that maybe the horrific ordeal had sent them both round the bend.

Once they had arranged to meet up the next day, Kat ended the call and threw a handful of soap bubbles at Jerry. He responded in kind, and within a few minutes the floor around their tub was soaked and covered in melting bubbles.

Kat leaned back in the tub, catching her breath while surveying the devastation around her, including their muddy clothes and discarded dishes lying amid puddles of water.

"Good thing this isn't the nice suite," said Kat quietly.

"Speaking of which," said Jerry, "might I be so impertinent as to ask, did you actually *purchase* this hotel? I caught a quick glance at the interim bill that Management so kindly slipped into your hand before we made our escape into the elevator, and at first I thought they'd accidentally passed you the GDP figures for some small island nation."

Kat was momentarily delayed in responding, as she was directing all her energies to fashioning a handlebar moustache out of soap suds. After a loud throat-clearing from Jerry, she looked over to him absent-mindedly.

"Hmm? Bill, you say? That's rather cheeky of them, don't you think? I mean, here we've barely darkened their doorstep and already they're shoving blasted accounting papers in our face. You'd think they'd at least have the decency to wait until morning, and then just discreetly slip the tally under our door after we're good and stuffed with coffee and bacon and English muffins. I've a good mind to—"

"Kat!"

"Jerry, please don't interrupt me dear, I was in the middle of formulating a perfect dressing-down to be delivered to that mousy little man at the front desk, and now you've gone and derailed my whole train of thought—"

"Kat!"

This last ejaculation startled her so much that the accumulation of soap suds was dislodged from her lip, which was a shame, actually, as it had begun to take on quite a convincing shape. Kat looked over at Jerry petulantly.

"Now look what you've done, Sahib. I spent a lot of valuable time and effort on that moustache.

"—And don't '*Kat!*' me, buster. Those peasants risked their lives to save mine, and it's certain that both their homes are nothing but ashes right now. The least – and I mean the VERY LEAST – we can do for them is put them up in some flophouse for a few days and buy them new rags to change into."

"By 'new rags'," said Jerry, "are you perhaps referring to the entries on pages four through eleven that prominently feature the nomenclatures, 'Versace', 'Chanel', 'Gucci', and 'Manolo Blahnik'? There are other names, as well, but you get the gist."

"Jerry, I don't care if they hired Rumpelstiltskin at his going rate to custom-weave garments out of spun gold, I won't hear another word about it." And she sank down out of sight under the water, leaving nothing but a single long lock of hair bobbing on the water's surface, looking for all the world like a defiant, undulating middle finger.

"Rumpelstiltskin's fee I could deal with," grumbled Jerry at the hirsute digit. "For what this hotel is charging, we could buy ourselves a dozen firstborns."

Kat's head bobbed back above the surface and she blinked a watery glare in his direction and said, "Hmm? What's that you say?"

"Nothing. Nothing at all," he replied, before sinking underneath the water himself. A wise man knows when to cede a point, and so did Jerry.

About an hour later, as Jerry reclined in the bath beneath a tray buckling under the weight of the dinner dishes, he reluctantly laid down the last of the rib bones, having sucked it clean of every shred of meat. Standing beside the tub and wrapped head to toe in a plush Turkish bath towel, Kat looked down at him in disgust.

"There are small children starving somewhere in the universe, and you have no shame following up a steak dinner by polishing off a full rack of baby back ribs? If I hadn't seen it with my own eyes I wouldn't have believed it."

"It's all in service of the Greater Good, baby," said Jerry, meditatively sucking a smear of barbecue sauce off his finger before plunging his hand into the soapy water. "I fasted for several days in that orbiting gulag. Aside from the IV drip, they fed me nothing. This was just what I needed. After all, I need to keep my strength up."

"'Greater Good'? 'Keep your strength up'? What service can you possibly intend to perform that necessitates the consumption of several thousand calories? Are you expecting to run a marathon?"

"Maybe only in the most figurative sense of the word, baby. Remember, food isn't the only thing I was deprived of up there," and he reached out and yanked off her towel.

Laughing, Kat exclaimed, "Oh, it all becomes clear now! And here I thought you were anxious to get some bed rest!

"Well, hon," she said, bringing her face down to his and giving him a delicate peck on the lips, "That's absolutely one 'Greater Good' I can agree is worthwhile. Just be sure you wash that barbecue sauce off your face before you get out — I don't want to have to take another bath tonight. Besides, I don't think the taste will go well with the crème brûlée I'm bringing to bed."

The splashing sounds that followed her exit from the bathroom made her giggle.

Now that's definitely the sound of a man scrubbing his face.

MORNING CAME far too soon. Kat's Slimlines had to all but yell in her ear before she finally stirred in bed, pressing her palms over her eyes and groaning mournfully.

"What time did you tell Slaäm we'd meet him," mumbled Jerry into his pillow, having been awakened by Kat's loud yawning and exaggerated stretching accompanied by one or more of her elbows or knees prodding rudely into him.

"I think we said 3pm."

"Three!" groaned Jerry. "Why didn't you just set it for dawn while you were at it?"

"Oh don't be such a drama queen," said Kat, groggily feeling around for the hotel phone. "You'll feel better once you've had a few gallons of coffee poured into you.

"I can't figure out these French," she continued, ear pressed to the handset. "Dinner they treat like their last meal before the Second Coming of Christ, but when it comes to breakfast, they act as though consuming a croissant and a boiled egg is tantamount to gluttony….

"Yes, hello? Room Service? This is— oh, you know already, right. Well, can you send up— oh, you already have something ready?... What's that?... Bacon, eggs, hash browns, muffins, tureen of oatmeal, sliced bananas, half grapefruits, French toast, flapjacks, two large carafes of coffee… yes, that sounds about right. How did you— yes, we're American…. Riiight. I'm not sure how to take that… Okay, send it up. And we need clothes, too…. No, of course I know you only serve food. Tell the clothes people to hustle their butts up here with our duds, unless you want to see us downstairs in our underwear…. Ha ha, very funny."

Hanging up the phone, Kat turned to Jerry and said, "You know, I think the anonymity of the Room Service dispatcher tends to induce impertinence."

Jerry didn't respond. He was snoring.

NOTWITHSTANDING THE HOTEL'S best efforts to overwhelm all their breakfast needs, Jerry and Kat had no trouble polishing off every single comestible item on the several trays of food which had been wheeled into their suite, and ended up arm-wrestling over the last muffin.

Kat finally abandoned the struggle and set herself to ripping open the packages of clothing that had been delivered while they dined. She was busy *oohing* and *aahing* over her new clothes while Jerry watched a news feed on the video wall in the bedroom.

"My God, Kat, you need to come look at this," called Jerry, his face ashen with horror. "Have you heard any of this news?"

"No, sorry – I'm pretty excited about all my new clothes. I'll have to make sure to intercept the bill before you catch sight of it…. Why, what's up, hon?"

"'What's up'? It's the End Times out there, Kat. Look at the chaos and frenzied crowds on this feed. The only thing missing is the Four Horsemen of the Apocalypse."

The video feed was coming from cameras mounted atop the walls surrounding the space station and displayed a panoramic vista stretching miles into the distance. The entire landscape was filled with surging crowds of panicked people, screaming hordes of weeping men, women and children hurling themselves at the walls of the Space Elevator complex.

At several spots along the wall, people could be seen hoisting themselves or their loved ones up and over, then disappearing out of view as they poured into the station's grounds.

As Jerry and Kat watched, openmouthed, one of the camera feeds was suddenly filled with the image of a huge tri-horned beast crashing into the throng of people and rampaging through the terrified multitude, leaving bleeding bodies and broken corpses in its wake.

The announcer on the feed was all but screaming into his microphone, calling out an anguished play-by-play as he related the swath of destruction created by the animal's passage through the mob. He made the reporter from the Hindenburg disaster seem calm and measured by comparison. Jerry half expected him to start wailing, "Oh, the humanity!"

Leaping out of bed, Jerry said, "Pack up all those lovely ensembles in your new luggage and get some clothes on, baby – we're getting out of here pronto. Within 24 hours this station will be overrun with refugees, and I want to be long-gone before then. Please tell me at least one of those outfits is for me. Even if none of them are, though, I'm still skedaddling, even if I have to do it in my skivvies."

"Um, yeah, Jerry – that stack over there is all menswear. And now I know the Apocalypse really has arrived – I don't think I've ever heard you tell me to put clothes *on* before...."

MATHILDE AND ELRIC were watching the video feed in their own suite, and were in an absolute tizzy when Kat came to get them.

"We all have to leave right away," said Kat. "I've already booked you passage on an Elevator leaving in two hours. The hotel is sending up a team of housemaids and footmen to pack up your new clothes and get your luggage onto the Elevator for you.

"Do you have your new passports and visas with you? Good. Go downstairs and the Manager will put you on a shuttle that will take you to your boarding gate. God Willing, I'll see you up there. Things will be a far sight calmer at the top. Very soon this entire facility will be absolute madness. You don't want to be here then."

"Aren't you coming with us, Miss Kat?" asked Elric.

"Jerry and I still have unfinished business to take care of down here," she said, not wanting to worry her friends by telling them it was quite possible there were orders out to assassinate her and Jerry if they were spotted in the terminal.

"I've booked us all a set of suites in one of the hotels in the space station. You'll be staying there until your interstellar transport to Agrus 9 leaves next week. We'll come join you when we get up to the station and we'll all laugh about this. But first the three of you need to board that Elevator. *Now*."

Mathilde's child scurried out from behind her mother's skirt and ran over to clutch Kat's leg, attaching herself like a remora and ignoring Mathilde's commands to remove herself.

"Bless her heart, she doesn't want you to leave again," said Mathilde. "Come back here, child! Miss Kat will see us again soon, don't you worry."

Looking up at Kat, she added quietly, "*I'll* do all the worrying for both of us."

Kat wrapped the woman in a huge hug and gave her a big kiss on the cheek, and then the two of them peeled the child's arms off her leg. As she and Jerry left the suite, she glanced back to see that it was taking both Mathilde and Elric to restrain the child from running after her again.

"That kid sure has taken a liking to you," said Jerry.

"I see that. And to think I didn't even have to feed her any smoked salmon," added Kat with an evil grin.

*   *   *

KAT AND JERRY slipped into the personnel corridors at the first opportunity. In all likelihood the Detention Facility had restored power and communications by now, and they were both probably marked as dangerous felons by the groundside authorities. Kat's Slimlines continued to mask their detection from the electronic surveillance system, but couldn't do anything about human observers on the lookout for them.

"Now that I think about it," said Jerry, as they hustled through the service personnel passageways, "I'm surprised no one came to our hotel this morning to drag us away."

"I didn't book those suites under our names," answered Kat. "I used our numbered accounts from Banque Genève. Even the hotel doesn't know our names. Once they saw the money tap open up they forgot about asking."

"I still wouldn't want to hang around there sipping martinis, though. I hope your friends get away in one piece."

"So do I, Jer – they've got our luggage."

"Kat! What a mercenary attitude! I'm disappointed in you."

"Oh really? And if I told you the couturière was kind enough to include a dozen different sets of silk lingerie for me, would that still be your position?"

Jerry's eyes widened momentarily and he said, "Quiet, Kat, I need to say a prayer that your dear friends make it off this rock safely – maybe you should call the hotel and order up a security escort for them."

Kat grinned and punched Jerry in the arm.

A red light was persistently flashing in the corner of Kat's vision and she frowned in concern.

"I think something's wrong – I've been trying to raise Slaäm but he's not picking up."

"He's not expecting us for a couple of hours – maybe he's in conference. Judging by the news feeds we saw, the whole station must be in chaos. I'm surprised you were able to get your friends on an Elevator."

"I used our VIP passes. I'm trying not to think about which poor souls got bumped by my reservations.

"But I'm still worried about Slaäm – I'm not getting any message or response at all on his line. It's as though his number doesn't exist anymore."

"Huh. You're right, that's not good. Be on your toes, baby, we're not out of the woods yet."

"That's putting it mildly, Jerry. I don't think we've even left the campsite. And we're headed directly into grizzly bear territory."

30

"**ELL, KAT?** Is the coast clear?"

Jerry was pressed up against a wall at an intersection of passageways where their hallway met the main corridor leading to the Engineering Department. Kat held her glasses out at arm's length and scanned down the length of the corridor around the corner.

"My Slimlines say there's nothing unusual in sight," she said, holding her finger against her ear and listening intently. "They're not picking up any furtive conversations or suspiciously loitering individuals. I think we're good to go."

Slipping her glasses back on, she turned the corner and headed towards the entrance to the Engineering Department, Jerry nervously trotting along behind her.

They were still about ten meters away when a massive explosion erupted from inside Engineering. The blast hurled Kat off her feet, smashing her backwards into Jerry. The back of her skull rammed into his face so hard it broke his nose. A hot barrage of broken concrete, cables, pipes, and various bits of machinery pelted them, accompanied by a hot wind that scorched their faces, followed by a thick cloud of smoke and soot that billowed into the corridor.

Ears ringing from the deafening roar that had accompanied the detonation, stumbling shapes blindly staggered through the chaos, collapsing or crawling on their hands and knees over the piles of debris filling the broad passageway. An ear-splitting shriek of alarms drowned out the moaning and screams of the survivors in the rubble.

Just then, the lights in the corridor all shut off, plunging the crowd of panicked survivors into even greater confusion. They reappeared in ghostly hues as the few scattered emergency lights clicked on simultaneously.

Pulling herself to her feet, Kat helped Jerry stand back up. His face was smeared with blood and he was bleeding liberally from his nose and forehead.

Kat looked like a cartoon monster, completely unmarked on her back, but black from head to toe with a thick blanket of soot coating her face and the front of her body.

"Oh my God, Jerry – we have to go in there and see if Slaäm survived that blast!"

He pointed to his ear and pushed the heel of his palm against it. Kat understood immediately that, if his eardrums hadn't actually been ruptured by the sonic boom from the explosion, his ears were at least ringing loudly enough to impair his hearing.

Kat's Slimlines had protected her from the worst aural effects of the blast by using her ear canal implants to cancel the sound waves before they could reach her eardrums. She nodded at Jerry, pointed to her own ear and gave him an "OK" sign.

On cue, the ceiling sprinklers all activated at once, drenching everyone with ice cold water.

"Ack!" coughed Kat. "This isn't helping at all!"

The soot ran down her face and clothing in thick clots as the water sprayed down, leaving a small river of muddy black gunk spreading out from where she stood.

"Take my hand, Jerry," shouted Kat into his ear. "We need to get to Slaäm's office. I can see perfectly in this mess. Thank God my Slimlines weren't blown off my head."

Stumbling forward, she led Jerry towards the Engineering Department when she felt an iron grip on her arm yanking her back as a rough voice growled at her, "No! Don't go in there! Come here, you two!"

Kat pushed Jerry away as she spun and straight-armed the man pulling her arm. He stumbled backwards then ducked as she launched a roundhouse kick at his face.

Spotting a broken pipe in the debris, she snatched it up and prepared to smash the man in the head, when he exclaimed, "Hey! No – cease fire, already! It's me! Wilkins! Remember? Slaäm sent me to watch for you!"

Kat froze in place and lowered the pipe, but kept gripping it threateningly. The torrent of water continued to stream down onto her through the thick black smoke swirling in the air like a torrential downpour ripping through a forest fire. But through her Slimlines Kat could see the man clearly, as he cowered on the ground in a defensive position in front of her.

"What do you mean?" she asked, yelling to make herself heard over the cacophony around them. "Why would Slaäm need you to be on the lookout for us?"

"Because he's not here – he's hiding in a safe spot. He wants me to take you to him!"

Kat's mind raced with possible choices. They needed to get to Slaäm, but could she trust that this man wouldn't be leading her into a trap?

Deciding she had no choice in the matter, she said, "Okay. We'll come with you. But I'm warning you, you don't want to mess with us. If you're not on the level you'll regret it."

"I believe you," said Wilkins, rubbing his neck where the heel of Kat's palm had jammed into him. "Slaäm told me to be careful approaching you. I just didn't think you'd react like a rabid puma."

"I've had a hard couple of days, okay? Count yourself lucky I missed your jaw with my foot."

Kat turned around and grabbed Jerry, who was having trouble peering in the darkness through the smoke and thick sprays of water still pouring from overhead.

"C'mon, Jer – Slaäm's not here, but our old friend Wilkins says he's going to take us to him. Take my hand and we'll get out of here."

Wilkins led them through the debris and the crush of people, which now included a stream of first-responders. Pawing his way through the smoke while he kept one hand on the corridor wall, he stumbled over the scattered debris until they were finally able to turn into a side corridor.

"Stay close to me," he told Kat. "If I lose track of you Slaäm will have my head."

As they moved farther away from Engineering, the crowds noticeably thinned out. Kat kept her Slimlines on full alert, setting them to scan for anyone paying closer than normal attention to them, as well as checking to make sure they weren't being followed. Her biggest advantage lay in the fact that her glasses could scan in a 360° circle without her turning her head. Any pursuers might get careless, thinking they were following unseen.

Jerry leaned close to Kat and said, just a little too loudly, "My hearing's coming back, Kat. There was a pretty loud ringing going on there for a moment, but I think I'll be okay."

"Look at the bright side, Jerry. Now when I tell you it's your turn to empty the litter box you can pretend you didn't hear me."

Wilkins led them through a stairwell access door and they climbed up several levels before emerging into a plain, white corridor with a series of numbered doors.

"Personnel offices," explained Wilkins. "Mostly unused, kept available for visiting staff who might need to come onsite for a week or two."

He stopped at one of the doors and tapped three times, paused, then repeated the knock. The door swung open and they were greeted by Slaäm's concerned face.

"Good Lord! What in the world happened to you two? Were you caught in that blast?"

Jerry's face was streaked with soot and smoke and thick smears of blood. Kat was blackened from head to toe.

"Ah, I gotta apologise, boss," said Wilkins. "They slipped past me somehow. I know you warned me they're tricky, but I was scanning every surveillance camera and they still got by. If I hadn't stepped into the corridor to get an in-person view for a moment, I wouldn't have seen them at all. As it is, they were about to enter Engineering when I spotted them. That's when the place went up."

"I told you they wouldn't show up on the cameras!"

"Yeah, but I thought you were exaggerating. I mean, it's not as though they can turn themselves invisible."

Pausing, he turned to look at Kat and Jerry.

"You, um, you can't actually do that, can you? Go invisible?"

"Only electronically," said Kat. "And don't give Jerry any ideas. I shudder to think of the places he'd go if he could turn himself invisible."

Jerry looked wounded, so Kat leaned over and gave him a kiss on the mouth.

"Yuck! You need to wash that face of yours, Jer! You taste like charcoal."

"You might want to take a look in a mirror before you start giving hygiene advice," replied Jerry.

Jerry turned to get a close look at the room they were in. There was a jury-rigged bank of monitors set up beside the desk, displaying various surveillance feeds from around the station, along with several with diagnostic screens, most of which were peppered with little flashing red alerts.

"What is all this, Slaäm?"

"My new command post. Wilkins and I set it up this morning when my phone stopped working."

"Yeah, what's the story there?"

"It saved my life, is what, when my phone suddenly went dead, along with all my other communications equipment. My computer went offline and I suddenly had no access to any video from the station, either surveillance or simple maintenance feeds.

"I had to literally walk over to IT to ask someone what was going on. I spoke with a nervous tech who stuttered out a garbled story about address conflicts and system reboots, but I could tell it was all bullshit.

"I didn't get really worried, though, until I got back to my office and noticed that several of my staff were conspicuously absent. I've always suspected there were spies in my department, but that never bothered me too much until this morning. Knocking out my phone and computer access put me on alert. So when I realised which personnel were missing, I knew what that meant and I couldn't collect my stuff fast enough before getting out of there.

"Luckily, I was able to find Wilkins and I enlisted his aid. We set up this office and tapped into the station feeds using a backdoor protocol. Then I sent him downstairs to intercept you two. And a great job he did there, too."

Wilkins looked down at the floor. The man was clearly in misery.

"This is bad, Slaäm," said Jerry. "It sounds like the foxes have taken over the henhouse."

"Only the basement, Jer. The attic is still safe. We just need to make it up the Elevator and then we can breathe easy.

"And I think it's a good sign that our enemies have gotten desperate enough to start setting bombs."

"Um, excuse me?" said Kat as she peered morosely at her reflection in a darkened monitor screen. "How do bombs going off around us qualify as a good sign?"

"Because it means the authorities still maintain some semblance of control, even down here. The bad guys wouldn't be rushing to eliminate us if they weren't concerned about us blowing the lid on their operation. The fact that they've resorted to mass destruction indicates their position isn't so invulnerable. That reinforces my belief that if we can make it to the space station we'll be safe."

"There's a big 'if' in that sentence, Slaäm," said Jerry.

"After that explosion, I think our chances got a lot better, Jer. I left my phone on my desk and when I slipped out I acted as though I was taking just a quick bathroom break. And for the last couple of hours Wilkins would occasionally poke his head into my office and talk loudly. Chances are, it will be at least an hour or so before the debris can be cleared away enough to search for my body. Until then, our enemies probably believe they got the job done. They might even think they got you two, as well."

"Why us?" asked Kat.

"I made sure to let it slip that I was expecting another visit from my offworld friends this afternoon. Except I moved the time up by a couple of hours. I got the idea from you, Kat, after our last lunch meeting. Sure enough, that explosion went off about ten minutes after you two were supposed to show up."

"You don't think anyone was curious why they never spotted us going in?"

"I think these people we're up against have figured out you guys know how to defeat the video surveillance system. And it's such a busy department, it's not inconceivable that you could have slipped in unnoticed, especially since the rats all fled the ship for fear of becoming collateral damage."

"I gotta admit, Slaäm, you seem to have covered all the bases, which leaves just one last hurdle."

"I think that's a mixed metaphor, baby," said Kat. Jerry gave her a look, and she winked back, grinning.

"I take it the 'hurdle' you're referring to is getting off this rock and back into space, right?"

"Precisely. We won't make it within fifty feet of an Elevator before someone drops a bag over our heads."

"That might be true for the *public* Elevators, Jerry, but I think Kat knows that's not the only way back up."

"Oh no!" wailed Kat. "Slaäm, please tell me you're not suggesting what I think you are!"

Slaäm chuckled and, without saying any more, just reached into a box and tossed Kat a plastic-wrapped sandwich and a diaper. She looked at him in horror as he broke out into a hearty guffaw.

"Time to suit up, you two! Wilkins has our transport all gassed up and ready to go."

Jerry looked at Kat questioningly and she just grimaced, then said, "The less you know, the better, Jerry. But you might want to pay a quick visit to the little boys' room before we head out – it's going to be a hard afternoon."

31

THEIR LITTLE GROUP darted stealthily along the passageways leading to the Elevator maintenance bays. Kat had added Slaäm and Wilkins to her counter-surveillance program, but they were still wary of every passer-by they encountered.

"I've never felt so vulnerable in these passages," said Slaäm. "I feel like every set of eyes is recording us and reporting on our movements."

"I think you can relax a bit, Slaäm," whispered Kat. "My glasses are running a diagnostic on every face we pass. Any unusual interest or suspicious facial responses will light up my alerts. So far, everyone's mostly ignored us, and there's no one following us, either."

"You don't think your being covered in muddy soot is a bit of a giveaway?"

"Since we've already passed a dozen other people who look like they've been working in a coal mine all morning: no."

They turned into a narrow, poorly-lit passage running off to the right that dead-ended about ten meters down, at a locked metal door with no markings.

"Okay, you guys wait here," whispered Wilkins. "This is an emergency exit from the maintenance bay, on the other side of this door. I'll go round and enter the bay by the main corridor. It shouldn't take more than sixty seconds for me to clear out any techs or mechanics working in there. Once the bay is clear, I'll come open this door."

Wilkins spun off and raced back up the little passageway, leaving the three of them waiting in the dead-end hallway.

"That's a real righteous guy you got there, Slaäm," said Jerry quietly, keeping a wary eye on the passageway leading back to the main corridor. "I hope his involvement in this affair doesn't come back to bite him in the ass."

"Not likely. Wilkins is the logical successor to my position. Since I'm leaving with you and Kat, I have a feeling he's looking at a big promotion in the immediate future."

"You mean the station isn't shutting down? Judging by the apocalyptic scenes we saw earlier today, I'd thought this whole shebang would be closing up within days."

"Oh, the planetside population will be leaving, there's no doubt about that. The last department heads meeting I had yesterday was all about moving the refugees into the station complex and then off-planet. We expect about fifty thousand may make it past the Goddaffulls, if they're lucky."

"That many?" asked Kat.

"Out of almost five hundred thousand current planetary residents, I'd say that's a pretty poor number."

Kat gasped and covered her mouth with her hand.

"And I'm responsible for that?" she asked, horrified.

"Don't beat yourself up about it. There's lots of reasons why this was inevitable. And don't forget that, for virtually all these poor souls who've been trapped in this Dark Ages gulag, life has been nothing but sheer, unadulterated misery for generations. Marooned in a feudal society as starving serfs, deprived of education, medical care, or the benefits of proper nutrition and hygiene, without any hope of breaking free, while the rest of the galaxy enjoys the best standard of living humans have ever known.

"And willingly kept that way by tremendous financial interests concerned only with lining their pockets."

"But all those lives—"

"Were only too happy to embrace deadly, savage entertainments and animal abuse as part of their culture. You reap what you sow, Kat."

"But that doesn't explain why this station will still be needed after the population has all been evacuated," said Jerry, hoping to move their topic of conversation away from the human carnage.

"Don't be naïve," said Slaäm. "This planet is still the most abundant source of halladium in the universe. The mining companies have been itching to shake off the onerous technology-averse restrictions they've been working under. They'll put up barriers around all the mining sites and probably triple production within months. I'm sure there's quite a few fat cats out there who'd like to shake your hands. What you two have done for them will increase their profit margin by double digits."

"Say," said Kat, "I don't like to be a Nervous Nellie, but shouldn't Wilkins have returned by now?"

"That's right. Slaäm, what do you think? Do we dare slip round to see wha—"

At that moment a harsh scraping sound came from the door, and then the sound of a latch being drawn back, followed by the door swinging open to reveal a badly disheveled Wilkins standing in front of them, holding his arm tightly against his side, a long stream of blood dripping down onto the floor from his hand.

"Oh Lord, what happened? Are you badly hurt?" Slaäm cried out.

"Relax, boss. It's just a small cut. I just need a tourniquet and I'll be aces."

Jerry looked at him skeptically. "Aces, eh? And how did you get this 'small cut'? By falling onto a machete?"

"Um, Jer," said Kat, looking past Wilkins's shoulder. "I think maybe one of those two bodies lying on the floor over there might have played a small part."

At the far end of the room, near its main entrance and just to the side of the control room, two large bodies lay face down, motionless. The one closest to the door had a badly twisted neck and his head lay at an unnatural angle. The other body looked unharmed, if you ignored the large pool of dark red liquid slowly spreading out from under it. Both men were clothed in long brown leather trench coats.

"They were waiting here when I came in. I told them they had to leave and… well, things went downhill from there. The first guy wasn't much trouble. I picked up a twenty-pound hex wrench, and he went down like a sack of potatoes.

"The second guy was a bit tougher. He had a blade. I guess I got careless." He looked down ruefully at his arm, where Kat was already busy tying a tourniquet from a strip of fabric she'd torn off Jerry's t-shirt. "He got me when I tried to grab his wrist. But when he tried to yank his blade back out I thought I'd save him the trouble and I removed it for him, and then I returned it to him."

"You sound pretty capable for an engineer," said Jerry. "I would have thought you'd be more at home with graphs and a slide rule."

"I served in the Navy for five years before I came here. You pick up skills," he said with a little grin.

"But this opens up a whole new can of worms," said Slaäm. "When these guys don't report back, this maintenance bay will be ground zero for our new playmates. We'll never make it up to the station in time."

"Relax, boss. I got this covered. I can disable the control room so no one can mess with the maintenance Elevator once it's underway. These two guys are the only ones who saw me, and they won't be telling anyone about it. I can slip back into Engineering and make it look like I was injured in the explosion."

"Uh-uh. No way I'm getting in an Elevator with no controls," said Slaäm. "I'd rather take my chances down here than freeze to death hanging from a cable."

"You will have controls, though, Chief."

Turning to Kat, he said, "Those glasses of yours – they can operate the Elevator, right?"

"Um, well, I haven't tried, but if you can get me access, then yeah, I suppose so."

"There," said Wilkins, turning back to Slaäm. "As long as you don't mind letting a girl drive, problem solved."

"I'm not sure how to take that comment," said Kat. "I'm considering punching you in your bad arm, just to be safe."

Wilkins just laughed and wrapped Kat up in a big bear hug.

STILL DON'T LIKE THIS," muttered Slaäm as they strapped themselves into place in the maintenance Elevator.

"Oh, lighten up, Slaäm," said Jerry cheerfully. "You didn't think Kat could get us back from the prison facility in two maintenance bots, either."

"And look how well that went. You're not really improving your case here, my friend."

"Relax, Slaäm. I got this," said Kat, frowning through her glasses. "Although the controls seem unnecessarily complex to me."

"My God, woman – you're driving a 5,000-kilogram box up a thin cable sixty thousand kilometers long! And at no time will there be any physical connection to the wire, if you don't count the tremendous electromagnetic forces that will be both tethering us to the line and pushing us up into space. And we have to precisely calibrate our acceleration and deceleration or we run the risk of overshooting our landing and sailing off into the cosmos."

"Now you're just being silly, Slaäm. I know that won't happen. The station is shielded at the top end. No way we'd break through. We'd just be crushed into pulp."

Slaäm turned to Jerry with a look of exasperation and disbelief.

"Hey, don't look for support from me, Slaäm. I learned my lesson back when she loaded me into a metal coffin in my underwear and dropped me into the void. At least now I get to die fully dressed."

"WHOA!" yelled Kat, as the Elevator bucked viciously and thrust them back into their seats. "Holy crap, these controls are really sensitive!"

"Wait, Kat, honey – why are you messing with this thing? Wilkins is going to set the program. You shouldn't be doing anything right now."

"And I suppose you'd rather I learn what I'm doing when we're rocketing through the atmosphere, as opposed to some harmless experimentation right now?"

"Oh… right. Sorry. Go ahead."

"That's okay. I was only testing my access to the manual controls. Hopefully, my Slimlines will take care of everything without my intervention. Can't be too careful, though. Remember the Detention Facility."

"I have a feeling that's going to be our new mantra, sort of like, 'Remember the Alamo'," said Jerry.

"What's the Alamo?" asked Kat.

"Hopefully, not a good analogy for our present situation."

Wilkins came up to the Elevator door and poked his head in.

"It's go-time, folks. Slaäm, I'll talk to you when you're safe and sound upstairs. Jerry, Kat, it's been a pleasure."

"Really? 'A pleasure'?" asked Kat. "Wilkins, you really need to get out more."

Chuckling, he slid the door shut and disappeared, and a moment later they felt a soft tug as the Elevator lifted and slowly rose up the exit shaft.

Wilkins had programmed an eleven-hour trip for them up the wire, but they were only about five hours into their journey when the Elevator began a sudden deceleration.

"Uh-oh. What's going on, Slaäm?" asked Jerry.

"It's got to be the ground station. They can still affect our passage from the main control room. They can't actually jack into our controls, though, because our craft isn't part of the main system. But they can send false alerts that will activate the safety protocols and reverse our ascent."

"Kat?"

"Hold on, I'm working on it. The safety protocols are especially difficult to defeat. Every time I green-light one set of commands, another set shuts down. Just give me a moment."

"Better hurry, baby," said Jerry, as their seats began to swivel in response to the altered momentum of the Elevator.

"I'm getting such strong electromagnetic interference that my glasses are having trouble controlling all the systems. I forgot about the electronics problem on these things."

"This is a maintenance Elevator, though, Kat," said Slaäm. "We've specially shielded it with a few hundred kilo of copper mesh. Your glasses should still be able to function."

"They're working fine – it's your Elevator that's bitching, Slaäm. It's confused. I think I'm getting closer, though."

The Elevator shuddered, then started to pick up speed again, and their chairs swiveled back to their original positions, but then they were hit with another push of deceleration and their chairs swiveled again.

"Kat, I'm getting seasick here," said Jerry.

"Hey, patience, grasshopper. I'm almost there. I think I've found an administrative lockout that will let us do anything we want, safety be damned."

"Oh, good," muttered Slaäm mournfully.

"There! All done!" The craft picked up speed and their chairs did their little dance and changed their orientation once again.

"Only problem is, now we can't use any of the Elevator's operational programs – they are all subservient to the safety protocols. So it's time I get to see just what this baby can do!" And she cackled madly.

As they were pressed back viciously into their seats under a tremendous burst of acceleration, Slaäm looked over at Jerry with a pleading look in his eyes. Jerry just shrugged, then closed his eyes.

KAT LET HER SLIMLINES make all the calculations for their acceleration and deceleration, with strict instructions to keep them well below 4 Gs at all costs. They passed several of the public Elevators at such a high speed the other craft flashed by in a blink of the eye. They couldn't tell if the public Elevators were stopped or being forced to return to the planet in response to the spurious safety alerts in the system. Kat hoped that Mathilde wasn't stuck on one of them right now. Wouldn't that just be the icing on the cake for the little group, she thought. *First time off-planet and they're trapped in a suborbital yo-yo. They'll probably be traumatized for life.*

Once they had passed geostationary orbit, their speed picked up noticeably, but after about an hour the deceleration procedure kicked in. They gritted their teeth as they were pasted back in their seats.

"Last third of the trip," moaned Kat. "We're in the home stretch now."

"I could do with more 'home' and less 'stretch'," Jerry croaked.

THE LAST HOUR was especially brutal, and the trio gasped in relief when their Elevator finally settled into place in the space station.

"My God, we made it! I would have lost a lot of money on that bet," exclaimed Slaäm.

"You're welcome," said Kat. "I told you we'd have no problems. Don't forget to tip your driver as you exit the vehicle."

They released their seat harnesses and all three of them tumbled to the cabin floor.

"Ohhhh, I remember this feeling," groaned Kat. "Please, God, let me never agree to do this again. My next vacation is going to take place on a massage planet, if I have anything to say about it."

Slaäm looked over at her with amusement. "So you still consider this a vacation, do you? What do you do for work — jam needles into your eyeballs?"

Jerry staggered to his feet and leaned his weight into the door latch, rotating the gigantic wheel until he was able to release the locking mechanism and push the panel aside.

They stumbled out into the bay and stood there puffing heavily, trying to catch their breath and gather their senses. The maintenance bay was dark and deserted. No one had been apprised of their trip, so no personnel were on hand to handle the docking and unloading of the Elevator.

A variety of dim shapes filled the hangar: maintenance Elevators waiting to make the return trip to the surface, interspersed with huge robotic repair units scattered here and there, and a long line of small maintenance bots, each one sitting on its own small metal square outlined with an angry black and yellow dotted line. Jerry shuddered briefly at the memory, then turned to Kat and said, "Okay, babe, let's go home."

"Now there's a noble sentiment," came a deep voice from the shadows near the repair bots, as a large, heavyset man stepped out into a pool of light. "I almost hate to stick my nose in and ruin the party. Almost."

Jerry and Slaäm froze in place as they assessed this new player, but Kat seemed merely annoyed.

"Herie," she said flatly. "What are you doing here?"

"Why, waiting for you, Miss Kat. And what a pleasure it is to see you again. I was really quite worried about you after you set out on that rescue mission of yours.

"It was very clever of you," he continued, casually slipping his right hand into his suitjacket pocket, "to ask DeMarco to keep me available onsite in case you 'needed me'. Stuck here on the station, with all our comm links down, I had no way to warn my associates about you.

"All I could do was hope that an entire maximum-security prison was more than a match for one simple girl. And I have to admit, I'm a bit surprised you pulled it off."

"I'm sure you are," she said coldly. "I'm sorry to disappoint you."

"Um, Kat?" said Jerry. "Can you fill us in, please?"

"No, no – let me. I insist," said the big man. "It's so rude of me not to properly introduce myself. Neil Herie, GSC Chief of Station Security. At your service."

"I sincerely doubt that," said Kat, eyeing the pulse weapon Herie gripped in his right hand.

"Haw! This one sure is feisty, isn't she?

"By the way, Miss Kat, you really must tell me how you managed to kill all our comms – we still haven't been able to reestablish communications with the Detention Facility. It's been giving our technicians fits. They think a powerful AI is running in a hidden level in our system, but we can't track it down. It's not often we encounter such stellar technology. It will be quite a feather in my cap when I get to the bottom of it."

"Be sure and tell me how that works out for you. Now get to the point. What do you want?"

"Want? Why, very little, actually." And without saying anything further, he squeezed his finger and a long white blast of plasma shot out of his hand weapon and seared into Slaäm's body, burning a deep hole into his side.

Jerry dropped to his knee to grab Slaäm, and Kat prepared to leap at Herie. But the GSC man was out of reach, and he turned and pointed the weapon directly at Kat.

"Now, I'll make you a deal, little lady. I won't burn any more holes in your friends here, if you'll tell me what you've learned about our little smuggling operation. I'm especially interested in finding out if my name appears anywhere in that data file you deciphered. My payments went to an off-planet numbered account under my coded ID, but it only takes one idiot slipping-up to spill the beans.

"Of course, I'll also need to know how much you know about our procedures, and who the rat is who supplied that data file. And that little trick with our computer system, of course. Can't forget that one."

"Bite me."

"Oooh, bad choice of words," he said, and another long stream of plasma spit out and burned a fiery white line into Jerry's right shoulder.

Jerry shrieked in pain and fell backwards, collapsing onto Slaäm, who was still writhing in pain on the decking.

Kat clenched her fists and stood rigid, fiery rage written clearly on her face.

"Those are just little attention-getters," said Herie, grinning maliciously. "I don't mind taking my time with you three – you've already cost me so much.

"Or did you think your interference in our affairs was going to win you bouquets of roses?

"This was my *retirement,* you little bitch!" As he spoke he began to get more agitated, and his face darkened with red splotches.

"Ten *fucking* years I spent rotting in this godforsaken outpost, only to have some nosy, interfering little c—"

That was as far as he got before he suddenly tumbled backwards, almost cartwheeling away, bouncing and sliding across the decking, flailing frantically with his hands and arms, grabbing at pieces of machinery, cables, hoses, and every other protrusion he came across as he skittered uncontrollably across the deck toward the open hatch where a split-second earlier a maintenance bot had been parked.

Kat saw the hand blaster carom off various bits of machinery until it slid across the deck and disappeared into the vacuum of space.

Before Herie could make it to the gap, though, the hatch snapped shut, its programming instructing it to close up within seconds after releasing the maintenance bot.

The powerful force pulling Herie backwards suddenly snuffed out, and he came to a stop well short of the formerly open hatch.

He got to his feet painfully, glaring at Kat. Slowly and deliberately, he reached into the breast pocket of his suit jacket and extracted a large chunk of what looked like fudge. Popping it into his mouth, he said, "That's okay. I don't need a weapon to snap your little neck right off your nasty body. And then when I'm done with you, I'll show those two other idiots—"

This time, when Kat moved her jaw, she added a series of quick movements with her eyes, and not just one hatch, but all of them suddenly opened up behind Herie. The suction was so tremendous it pulled her off balance, too, even though she was a dozen meters farther than him from the hatches.

She watched as he was yanked off his feet and sucked inexorably backwards, finally disappearing through an open hatch. At the last moment, before vanishing into the inky blackness of space, he desperately grabbed at the lip of the decking, only to have the hatch snap back closed, neatly severing his fingers from the rest of him.

Four bloody stumps sat forlornly on the decking, resting on the angry yellow and black dotted line framing the words:

DO NOT STAND HERE

Jerry staggered over to Kat and wrapped his good arm around her, leaning heavily.

"Nice work, babe. A bit later than I'd have liked, but nice work, anyways."

"The bots' safety protocols kept blocking me – I had to route all my commands through the station mainframe. It took a minute."

She turned to assess Jerry's injury.

"Oh, Jerry! How bad is it? And what about Slaäm?"

"Not to worry, hon – both wounds are more painful than they are life-threatening. The plasma tends to cauterize the wound while it makes it. I don't think any of Slaäm's major organs were hit, and a quick trip to the medical bay should leave us both with nothing but a pair of fantastic scars to tell stories about in our old age."

"You're *already* in your old age, Jer."

"And look at all the new material I'm acquiring! I'll be an absolute font of fascinating stories for our grandchildren."

Kat snuffled in amusement, and buried her head in Jerry's shoulder. Outside, through the viewport, they could just barely make out the shape of a large, heavyset human being, slowly twisting in the frigid darkness of the endless night.

ARLA **DeMarco** tut-tutted reproachfully as she watched the medical bot working on Slaäm's wound.

"And to think I worked shoulder-to-shoulder with the man for years!" she groaned. "I feel like such an idiot."

"Hey, he was your Chief of Security. You had every reason to trust him," said Jerry quietly. "But money can make people do terrible things. Don't beat yourself up over it."

"I don't know how to thank you two. You did what we've been unable to achieve in years of trying."

"Again, not your fault. Herie was probably torpedoing every good lead you got, and alerting his confederates to your every move. If you think about it, the only way you were ever going to crack this thing was with complete outsiders, someone he couldn't reach. We may not have been willing participants, but we were exactly what you needed."

"Which leads us back to the million-dollar question," said the Station Manager. "I'm delighted to get the information you deciphered off that watch – we'll put away an awful lot of people with that data. But there's still one critical piece of information missing."

"You mean: 'how did they move the product out of orbit?' Right?"

"Precisely. Herie had no control over the station cargo inspections. We've got the who, what, where, but we're still in the dark when it comes to the how. And if we don't figure that out, the whole operation might start up again within days."

"Well, maybe as our parting gift, I can help you out with that, too," said Jerry.

Kat leaned back in her chair and watched Jerry with a wry smile on her face. She loved watching him when his inductive reasoning skills were on display. She understood how Dr. Watson must have felt.

"Something one of the guards in the Detention Facility said to me caught my attention. He was talking about the Death Match participants.

"What do you do," he asked DeMarco, "with the participants who lose? How do you dispose of their bodies?"

"Well, we try to give them as much dignity as we can, of course. I don't approve of the event, but I can't stop it. But we were able to insist that the deceased receive a proper burial – as much as can be achieved in space, of course. The corpse is sealed in an airtight capsule and delivered to a launch facility here on the station. We then jettison it into space. A small booster pushes the capsule out of orbit and off into the void. It's the best we can do for them."

"So then why would one of the guards have mentioned he gets the heebie-jeebies when he sees the bodies pushed out the airlock into space?"

"I can't imagine what he would mean by that."

"Let me spell it out for you," said Jerry. "There are no bodies in those capsule-coffins. Instead, they are filled with a hundred kilos of Agresso and a time-delayed tracking device, and picked up a few days later by a passing ship.

"The actual bodies are just chucked out of an airlock and eventually get torn to shreds by the planet's powerful atmospheric storms."

"But what you're describing," said DeMarco, "would require a coordinated effort involving dozens of ships, since there's a Death Match every week, each with several participants. And, while we do have a wide range of ships passing in and out of orbit on a regular basis, they would all have to be involved in a massive, complex and ongoing conspiracy. That would be impossible to keep quiet for very long."

"Not if it were all being done by a single company, operating with a handpicked staff. Maybe someone with an exclusive contract to provide certain services to the Station."

"But who…."

Silently, Jerry reached into his pocket and pulled out a small flyer he had picked up while passing through the station. On the flyer was a picture of a cartoon pilot leaning out the window of a cartoon spaceship, smiling and waving.

"They make dozens of trips into and out of orbit every week," he said quietly. "The same ships, with the same pilots, and I'm sure every one of them is very well paid."

DeMarco looked up at him in amazement, then said slowly, "And they've had an exclusive contract with the station for the last…."

"Fifteen years or so?" offered Jerry. "That would fit the timeline pretty nicely, wouldn't it?"

DeMarco just nodded.

"And I'll bet Herie was in charge of vetting the background checks on the pilots, right?"

Another nod.

"Miss DeMarco, I think our work here is done."

Kat clapped her hands in pleasure.

"Bravo, Jerry! Another stellar performance!"

"Thenk yoo, thenk yoo," said Jerry, giving a little mock bow.

DeMarco looked at them wide-eyed.

"Do you two do this all the time?" she asked.

"Only when we're on vacation," said Kat, grinning.

34

KAT SETTLED BACK into her copilot's chair, running her fingers through Batman's fur while Jerry delightedly took his own chair through the full range of adjustments.

"Slaäm, your guy did a great job! This thing is moving even smoother than it did when it was new. That fellow deserves a promotion."

"It was a woman, Jerry, and she's already head of station-side maintenance. She worked on your chair as a personal favour to me."

"In that case, I'm even happier to ferry you wherever you want to go, my friend. Which reminds me – exactly what do you have in mind now that you're unemployed?"

"The Disney planet, Jerry. They reached out to me for their VP of Engineering position – seems that my time spent tending to the Space Elevator was a perfect preparation for running some of the galaxy's *second*-biggest thrill rides."

"Oooh, so if we visit," cooed Kat, "you can get us VIP passes to the attractions?"

"Um, well, I think I'd prefer it if you waited a couple of years before you came by, Kat – trouble seems to cling to you two like stink on a skunk. Can I have at least a few months to enjoy my new job before you drop in and reveal some big rum-smuggling operation run by the Pirates of the Caribbean?"

Kat grimaced. "That hurts, Slaäm. But only because it's so true."

Jerry stretched his hand out in front of him and admired his wrist.

"You really like your new watch, eh, Jerry?" said Kat.

"Sure do! It was awfully nice of DeMarco to let me keep the spy watch – it's even nicer than that fake Patek Philippe I've been sporting. And this one is real."

"As far as you know."

"Good enough for me," he said contentedly. "It was free."

"Speaking of which, I noticed you scanning our latest bill from the station, Jer. Please don't tell me you're going to obsess on every little charge."

"Can I at least obsess on those with more than four digits in their numbers?"

"Only if you promise to keep in mind the reward money the station gave us for busting that smuggling ring for them – I'm not sure, but I think we might even have turned a profit on the whole affair. Even including the cost of purchasing an Apothecary shop for Mathilde and Elric on Agrus 9."

"I don't begrudge you that, Kat. I'll consider it their wedding present. Besides, it's not as if you came out of this deal empty-handed yourself."

"What do you mean?"

"Oh, don't play dumb with me, baby. I know full-well why you wanted to tag along when Security searched Herie's quarters, and then had DeMarco walk you back to our ship. Don't think I missed what you stuck in the freezer when we got back here. And don't even bother trying to tell me it's fudge. That brick must weigh five kilos, minimum. I'll have to make you pee in a cup before we spar in the mornings."

"I'm sure I have no idea what you're talking about," said Kat innocently.

The little black and white cat sitting on her lap looked up and said, "Mrow."

"Not even Batman believes you," said Slaäm, laughing.

"You can't trust his opinion," said Kat. "He's just pissed at being locked in here alone for the last two weeks."

"Well maybe this will cheer him up," said Jerry excitedly. "Now that we've got network access again, I see that one particular event from the last Tourney has gone viral across the galaxy."

The blood drained out of Kat's face. "Jerry! NO! Please don't tell me what I think you're going to tell me!"

"Oh *yes*, honey. That little stunt we pulled in the arena was streamed live to all sixteen hundred settled planets. It's already topped thirty billion hits on U-tube! You're famous, baby!"

"Oh! Let me see!" said Slaäm, grabbing Jerry's phone.

"Look!" said Jerry excitedly, as he and Slaäm bent their heads to peer at the display. "Watch this – here's the part where she starts squealing "SQUEEE!"

Both men roared in laughter as little high-pitched "squeee"s screeched from the phone speakers.

"Play it again! Play it again!" said Slaäm. "Oh my God, that's absolutely classic!"

Horrified, Kat stood up and stomped out of the cabin.

"While you're having fun with your little entertainment, I think I'll be relaxing in the hot tub. Come on, Batman. Let's leave the children to their juvenile amusement."

The sounds of the two men's rollicking laughter followed her through the ship. As she stepped into the tub and sank down into the water, she could hear Jerry exclaiming, "Ooh ooh, this part's great – it's where the Goddaffull dumps the first big load of snot onto her – wait for it… here it comes… OHHHHHH!"

"You know, Batman," she said, sinking lower into the water, "Some days it just doesn't pay to get out of bed.

"But don't worry – we'll have the last laugh on them. Just wait till Jerry sees how much first-class interstellar transportation costs for a horse."

Chuckling evilly to herself, she sank beneath the surface while the little cat sat on the edge of the tub, watching the bubbles pool on the water.

Did you enjoy this book?

If you did, then I'm delighted!

And if you'd like to see more like it, there's one simple little thing you can do for me that's worth its weight in gold (metaphorically-speaking):

Scan this code to leave a review!

Your online review will do more for me than you can imagine, and ultimately it will enable me to continue writing more books.

Plus, because I read every review, your review will help me to understand what you liked about my book, so that I can create others that you might enjoy even more!

THANK YOU, in advance.

--*J.M. Holmes*

ACKNOWLEDGMENT

Although space elevator technology is purely theoretical at the present time, the hard science behind it is very real. I am grateful to my clever fellow Canadian, Brian Eldridge, for his generous donation of time and expertise in assisting me in working out many of the calculations on the speeds and G-forces involved.

Brian is an engineer, but we shouldn't hold that against him. If nothing else, he is living proof that there is more to Canada than whores and hockey players.

(Before anyone gets upset by that last comment, let me explain that it is a line from a well-known classic joke. I can't take credit for it. If you're unfamiliar with the joke, just surf over to *jm-holmes.com* and you can find it there in full.)

But as long as we're discussing whores and hockey players, I need to recognize my Editor, Lee Zimmerman, whose participation in the creation of this book has been of inestimable value.

Lee may be woefully ignorant about Star Trek and many other cultural touchstones, but when it comes to polishing prose and gerrymandering grammar, he has no equal. I am always grateful to hand over my carefully constructed literary creations to his editing chainsaw; the resulting carnage may be a crime against Nature, but I begrudgingly admit that the final version is indisputably better than the unbutchered draft.

I fully expect to outlive him, and the only sombre note that will temper that joyous day's revelry will be the sad realization that, alas, he will no longer be able to elevate my scribblings to the level of perfection that everyone now expects. So eat your greens and get your exercise, Lee, because I've got a lot more writing to do!

about the illustrator

Francesco LaCerva was born more than half a century ago in Palermo on the beautiful island of Sicily, where he lives to this day.

A childhood immersed in films, cartoons, books and comics inspired him to bring to life drawing – first on the walls of his house, and eventually on sheets of paper – the fantastic characters and worlds of fantasy and science fiction.

Today Francesco supports his family, including three children, by working as an established architect. But between his daily commitments designing houses and other buildings, he still feeds his soul with a regular diet of books, comics, cartoons, and film. And ever faithful to his First Love, he dedicates his free time to illustration, never forgetting the passion that has always inspired him: drawing.

See more of his work at: *https://www.artstation.com/lacerva_art* or *https://www.deviantart.com/francescolacerva* or find him on *Instagram: @francesco_lacerva*

Francesco La Cerva nasce più di mezzo secolo fa a Palermo, nella bellissima isola della Sicilia, dove vive ancora oggi.

Un'allegra infanzia passata tra film, cartoni animati, libri e fumetti, lo hanno ispirato a riportare in vita disegnando, prima sui muri di casa sua e infine su fogli di carta, i fantastici personaggi e mondi immaginari di fantasy e fantascienza.

Oggi Francesco sostiene la sua famiglia, compresi tre figli, lavorando come un affermato architetto. Ma tra i suoi impegni quotidiani nella progettazione di case e altri edifici, nutre ancora la sua anima con una regolare dieta di libri, fumetti, cartoni animati e film. Sempre fedele al suo Primo Amore, dedica il suo tempo libero all'illustrazione, senza mai dimenticare la passione che da sempre lo ispira: il disegno.

Per vedere altri suoi lavori visita *www.artstation.com/lacerva_art* o *www.deviantart.com/francescolacerva* o visita su *instagram: @francesco_lacerva*

about the author

J. M. Holmes was born and raised in Canada
and educated in the Classics by Jesuits and nuns.

Amateur beekeeper, film historian, long-distance bicyclist,
author, computer whisperer, and the one person
who knows how to fix all the world's problems,
Holmes stubbornly defies categorization.

Especially proud of daughter Sarah and son Alex,
Holmes considers everything else in an admittedly
long and highly rewarding life as mere dross,
agreeing heartily with Ezra Pound, who points out:

> *What thou lovest well remains,*
> *the rest is dross.*
> *What thou lov'st well shall not be reft from thee*
> *What thou lov'st well is thy true heritage.*

(Including cats, of course.)

If you'd like to know more about the author,
read about upcoming (or past) books,
or offer your own comments,
direct your browser to:

jm-holmes.com

ADVENTURE IN ASTEROID CITY

Kat & Jerry are back!

Join Kat & Jerry on a nail-biting treasure hunt
at the far edge of the universe

A priceless artifact, hidden in a mining settlement
on an asteroid ring at the edge of colonized space.
It's another roller-coaster thrill ride adventure with
the galaxy's most entertaining pair of amateur sleuths!

This exciting cloak-and-dagger thriller will have you alternately
laughing along with these entertaining lovers or holding your breath
in suspense. It's a mix of action, suspense and humour that will
leave you hungry for more.

ICE, ICE, BABY

Don't miss this volume of three exciting scifi novellas

The ice will swallow the whole science station within days if Vedana, Alice, and their fellow scientists can't find out what's causing its unstoppable growth.

In the meantime, they're slowly being roasted to death by a malfunctioning life support system aboard their ship. If they don't restore the environmental controls they will be forced to evacuate to the planet's frozen surface.

And while they fight to avoid being frozen or cooked, a murderous saboteur bent on destroying their mission is killing them off one by one.

This thrilling scifi tale of two brilliant heroines leading their comrades in a life-and-death struggle will engage you from the very first page and leave you hungry for more.

VEDANA COULD HEAR the keypad beeping quietly as someone entered the door access code sequence. A metallic *click!*, a pause, a hiss, and she heard a footstep inside the room.

She would have bet money that her breathing could be heard throughout the whole ship, it seemed so loud to her. She opened her mouth wide and tried to calm her racing heartbeat, which was humming along at around 200 beats per minute.

She heard the footsteps moving quietly about the room, but they weren't wandering around aimlessly. Whoever they belonged to knew where to go and what to do. There was a quiet efficiency at work here. She heard a few little clinks, a quiet hum of some unknown machine, and the ripple of a zipper being opened and then, a second later, closed.

And then… silence.

Vedana froze. Had she done something to give herself away or left some tiny sign of her presence here?

The intruder seemed to be standing still in the dark lab.

Listening? Examining the room? What was he doing?

Vedana wanted to scream, the tension was so extreme.

And then she heard a quiet footstep come closer to her.

Then another.

The footsteps stopped directly in front of Vedana's cabinet.

She gritted her teeth, and waited for the inevitable yanking open of the cabinet door.

from THEY LEFT ME FOR DEAD:

THEY LEAVE ME for dead, lying in a drainage ditch beside the road, and I can hear them as they drive away in my car, just a couple of good ol' boys lighting cigarettes and cracking jokes, as though they're coming back from a fishing trip and not from having just beaten someone to death.

I can't tell you how long I lie here, listening to the rain and the wind and the crickets and all the assorted night sounds that creep back to life after the humans have gone. The stentorian gasps of my own ragged breathing keep time with the persistent rustle of some weeds just off to my left, making me wonder if perhaps some hungry wild creature is assessing my potential as a snack.

I am slipping into and out of consciousness every few minutes, and in a grey recess of my mind I peripherally hope that I will be insensate when the beast finally starts gnawing on whichever part of my body it's going to eat first. Every so often a vehicle shoots by in the night, announcing itself with the quiet hiss of its approach, then gradually crescendoing into a deafening, rattling roar defining its identity as car, pickup truck, or 18-wheeler. The weeds around my head sway and buck convulsively as the vehicle whizzes past my location, and then resume their motionless witness to my suffering.

I have no way to alert the passing drivers to my presence. I can't seem to move my arms and legs, or even turn my head, either because some part of my spine is damaged or because the intense pain from the rest of my body is overwhelming all my other senses. I know that several of my ribs are broken, along with at least two of the fingers on my left hand. My sides throb in excruciating pain, and I assume I'm bleeding internally from several damaged organs. I can't really see at all from either of my eyes, as both are swollen shut and caked in blood. The taste of blood fills my mouth and I can't breathe through my nose.

I lie here, face down in the dirt and muck, and I wait – for death, or the dawn. I wonder which will arrive first.

Literati International is the privately-held parent company of Literati Media, established in 1984 in Toronto, Canada, which comprises Literati Worldwide Publications, Literati Broadcasting Enterprises, Literati International Reporting & Podcast Productions, and Literati Film and Television Post-Production Services.

Literati International has affiliate partnerships and representatives in numerous countries around the globe, including Australia, India, and Brazil.

Check out the full line of Literati-produced books and media at www.literatiinternational.com

ARROW DELIVERIES
The Fastest Line between
any two points!